Robert Wanlock

Moorland rhymes

Robert Wanlock

Moorland rhymes

ISBN/EAN: 9783337264925

Printed in Europe, USA, Canada, Australia, Japan

Cover: Foto ©Andreas Hilbeck / pixelio.de

More available books at **www.hansebooks.com**

MOORLAND RHYMES.

BY

ROBERT WANLOCK.

(REID.)

DUMFRIES:

JOHN ANDERSON & SON, HIGH STREET.

1874.

GLASGOW:
PRINTED BY ROBERT ANDERSON
22 ANN STREET.

SCOTTISH POEMS.

CONTENTS.

SCOTTISH POEMS.

ENGLISH POEMS.

SONGS.

SONNETS.

DEDICATION.

TO JOHN MATHIESON REID.

Short syne, in the gray o' the dawin',
   Or Wanlock had opent its een,
When barely a muircock was crawin',
   And never a whaup tae be seen;
When even the laverock was sleepin'
   Abune the burn heids I gade through,
And ilka bit fitroad was dreepin'
   And drookit wi' dew,—

A

I gethert a hamely wee posie
   O' a' the hill blossoms in prime,
And buskit it trigly and cozy
   Wi' orra bit ravlins o' rhyme:
And kennin that ocht frae that quarter
   Wad gledden yer heart thro' and thro',
I yoked wi' the Musie and gart her
   Address it tae you.

Some bards get their sangs dedicated
   Tae big folk, tae gie them a heeze,
But gyte wad I be gin I waited
   Till big folk took notice o' these—
Wauf glisks o' the muirlan' and mountain,
   Odd blinks o' the corrie and glen;
It's little on favours I'm countin'
   For these frae sic men.

Their coach rumbles on owre the highway,
  And little its occupants care
What ferlies may lirk in ilk byeway
  That leads tae the moss and the muir;
What lilts o' the laverock and linty,
  What perfume o' brier and brume,
What wiels the wee burn popples intae—
  Ne'er fashes their thoom.

But you that were bred amang heather,
  A bird o' the muirs like mysel'—
And aften hae roved them tae gether
  The primrose and bonnie blue-bell:
Ye ken the lane scene o' ilk ditty,
  Glengaber, Necony, Glencrieve—
And far in the reek-ridden city
  Betimes ye may grieve

For a lown cannie oor in the gloamin'
    Tae breathe the sweet air o' the glens,
And listen the mavis while roamin'
    Away amang fairy-like dens:
And sae tae mak' short wi' your grievin',
    As far as sic substitute gangs,
I send you this wab o' my weavin'—
    This posie o' sangs.

And gin the wild ring o' their measure
    But wauken a thocht in your min'
O' the days when we feastit on pleasure
    I've ne'er kent the like o' sinsyne:
Gin Wanlock be onything dearer
    For ocht I hae mintit or sung,
And heather and bracken lie nearer
    Your heart and your tongue:

DEDICATION.

Gin the bonnie green howms o' the Mennock

    But ance in the fancy ye see,

Or rest by the linn o' Petrennock

    Heart-eased wi' its auld-warl' glee :—

Thir sangs o' mine bauldly may shaw them

    Though learned folk lichtly them sair :

What care I though critics misca' them ?

    I ettlet nae mair.

WANLOCK.

Did ye ever hear tell o' a lanely wee toon,
Far hid amang hills o' the heather sae broon,
Wi' its hooses reel-rall, keekin' oot at ilk turn,
Like an ill-cuisten crap in the howe o' the burn;
Ane here and ane there, wi' a fitroad atween,
In the daftest construction that ever was seen?

O there the cauld winter first comes wi' his snaw,
And he likes it sae weel that he's laith tae gae 'wa;
For there's three months o' bluister tae ilk ane o' sun,
And the dour nippin' cranreuch's maist aye on the
  grun':
Ay, whyles the corn's green in the lallans, they say,
Or the hinmaist snaw-wreath dwines awa' on the brae.

Frae mornin' till nicht ye wad tentily gang,

And no hear the cheep o' a hedge-sparrow's sang,

Nae merle at e'enin' his melody starts

Tae wauken the dream in the lassies' bit hearts,

But a corbie's maybe, or some ither as stoor,

Comes by wi' a wauf o' the win' frae the muir.

Then for flow'rs and sicklike, there's juist no sic a
      thing,

Except a wheen gowans a while in the spring;

And the twa-three bit busses the bodies ca' trees

Hae an auld-farrant look as they bend in the breeze,

And scarce want the gift o' the gab tae proclaim

They reckon this solitude ocht but their hame.

But, dod, for a' that its a wonderfu' toon,

There's hardly the like o't for parishes roon;

Though far frae a' neebors, and stannin' its lane,

Like a mitherless laddie left oot in the rain.

Ye'd open yer een, like a gled's tae the mune,

Gin ye kent a' the uncos its offspring hae dune.

For the chiels are as likely a set as ye'd meet

Frae the muir and the glen tae the square and the street;

Big, buirdly, and bauld, like the hills o' their hame,

And no cruppen doon wi' inherited shame;

But gaun frae the knee tae their grave in the glen,

Like their faithers afore them, the walins o' men.

And the lassies—preserve us! I'm fleyt tae begin,

Lest ony auld carles, wi' prejudice blin',

Should ever but hint sic anither wee place

Could brag o' sic beauties in figure and face:

Sae winsome and backward they were, for ye ken

That a' things were backward up there—but the men.

And 'deed, when I think on't, this very complaint

Was likely eneuch the best frien' that they kent,

For in love or in war the maist likely tae speed

Is the ane that first raxes for what he may need;

A laggard in poortith a lifetime may dwell,

But Providence helps him that's guid tae himsel'.

And let a' the virtues beside it be theirs,

'Twas weel eneuch kent o' thir men o' the muirs,

That blateness or backwardness ne'er was the thing

That keepit them quate when a ploy was in swing;

They'd face up tae onything comin' tae han',

And fecht for the brag wi' the best in the lan'.

For instance, I've heard o' a parish quite near

That keepit the causey at curlin' ae year,

And, tired o' defeatin' a' comers ablow,

Were braggin' o' gaun tae the mune for a foe,

When some ane suggested the victors suld try

A bout wi' the lads o' the muirlan' gaun by.

They did, and the consequence was that they fun'

They were matcht withoot gaun tae sic far-awa' grun;

For they left the heich kintra far sadder, we ken,

And wiser, we howp, than they cam' tae the glen,

Wi' their prood Suthron hearts like tae loup frae the

　　shawp,

And their fine balloon journey a' knockit tae jaup.

And that's but a swatch o' the plaiks that they play—

Be it curlin' or quoitin' they carena a strae:

In city or kintra their marrows are few

At ocht that'll bring the reid blude tae the broo;

And he that wad twine the free saul tae his will

Maun alter his thochts o' the men o' the hill.

And that's no the best o't—for nae bit I've been

Sic hamely, intelligent faces are seen:

Sae little they ken o' the ill warl's ways

That happiness lies like a dream on the braes;

And the lown cannie life o' the muirlan' gangs by,
The bud that will blossom or lang in the sky.

And better than that—if a better could be—
That howe in the heather is a' things tae me;
For there I first lookt on the licht o' the day,
Pree'd the first cup o' pleasure unmingled wi' wae,
And slum'd through the years o' my bairntime in glee,
As blithe as the linty that chirm'd on the lea.

There, tae, the first whisper o' heaven did start,
When the gowd dream o' love creepit in on my heart,
And there on the wild heather mountain I roved
Wi' the frien' o' my choice, like a lassie beloved;
But the tane is forgotten, the tither has fled,
And a licht less will glint on the muirlan' than did.

But O ! there are plenty tae welcome me still
When I follow my heart tae its hame on the hill;

Leal looks frae the auld, and kind words frae the young,

And the grup o' the han', that says mair than the

tongue;

And mony blithe memories wauken in me

Whenever the bloom on the heather I see.

Ye powers that can see through the maskins o' men,

Gin this be a lee, or the contrar' ye ken,

That never by mountain or valley hae I

Sic glimpses o' gladness and stounins o' joy,

Nae happiness ever beguiles me sae pure

As I pree when the gloamin' comes doon on the muir.

Sangs tell aboot Yarrow and Doon's bonny braes,

The Luggie rows saft in that measure o' Gray's;

Frae Tweed tae the Beauly there's hardly a glen

But brags it has minstrels and rhymes o' its ain:

Yet here's a wee toon never named in their glee,

That's mair than them a' put thegither tae me.

KILMENY'S WARNING.

I ferlied aft that wit and will
  Suld smoor aneth the gruesome grave,
And hoo nae crank o' mortal skill
  This deidly weird could save.

And whiles I thocht some baulder wing
  Micht cleave the mirk and come again,
Wi' posies o' the floors that spring
  Ayont the midnicht main.

Sae lang this howp my heart had fill'd,
  That howp a demon passion grew;
And late and air I socht and thrill'd
  Tae pruve my fancy true.

And pangt wi' fowth o' fearsome lair,
   I wrocht wi' candle, book, and bell;
Nae moil was hain'd that I could wair
   Tae work the faery spell.

But ane by ane ilk rede was thrawn,
   The wab I warpit wadna weave;
And fient an icker rowthly sawn
   Cam' stowlins tae the sieve.

Then tae the airts I bann't the book,
   And oot I sten't in thrawart dule,
Tae streak me in some lanesome neuk,
   And geck at fate, and snool.

Or, aiblins, doon the jinkin' burn,
   I'd dauner when the mune was fu',
Where halflin swankies blithely turn
   Tae sport wi' them they lo'e.

And this I lo'ed and grient tae grip,
    Cam' never till the sun was low;
Nor or the whitely mune was up,
    And a' was lown ablow.

Syne in the toom or dernest shaw,
    Through a' the eerie oors o' e'en,
I'd watch until the mornin' daw
    Tae see the fatal green.

But never glisk o' faery face,
    Nor morrice dance, nor witchin' spell,
Could I wi' a' my watchin' trace
    But this that noo I tell.

And suld the ferlie seem to some
    Nocht better than a daffin' skair,
It maksna, since the voice will come
    Amang oor glens nae mair.

Yestreen, when a' my darg was dune,
   And cankert care had loot me be,
I left yon waukrife wastlin' toon,
   Kilmeny's grave tae see.

Sae lown a gloamin' seldom creeps
   Atween the darkness and the day,
Sic eldritch light but seldom steeps
   The warlock's eerie brae.

By this I guess'd that verra nicht
   The morrice wad be danced again,
And ettled weel tae see the sicht
   Kilmeny saw alane.

The lift, a' whaur the sun had fa'n,
   Was reider than the burstit rose,
Though east and wast thegither drawn
   Begoud in murk tae close.

Yon hill, athort its yethert broo,
   Yet woo't the glint sae wae tae lea',
And doon this dowie hollow threw
   Its shade on burn and tree.

Lane muirlan' music fillt the air—
   Sae sweet tae me, that seldom heard
But orra liltins here and there
   O' lamb, or bee, or bird.

On ilka cairn the lintie sang,
   Frae spretty cleuchs the grey curlew,
And wilyart muircocks birr'd alang,
   And clapp'd their wings, and crew.

I couldna lowse the witchin' spell
   The time and place thegither brung,
It seem't the verra scene itsel'
   The shepherd poet sung.

Sae there, aneth the hoary haw,

    And as the win' was lownin' doon,

And gloamin' had begoud to draw

    A rowk owre sicht and soun',

I lay and croon't the bonnie sang—

    Hoo sweet Kilmeny left her hame,

And hoo her minny grat sae lang

    Tae see her clear o' blame.

Sma' need had I tae spell and glowr;

    It's lang sin' first it drew my min',

And aft I've rhymed it owre and owre

    In mony a glen sin' syne.

The glamour't lass—the minny's dule—

    The aftercome—I min't it a';

And thocht cam' thick as drift at Yule

    Aneth that hoary haw;

Till ane by ane ilk sicht and soun'
  Turn'd unco tae my dwaumin' brain,
And licht and landscape grew aroun'
  O' ither warlds again.

Here where the mawkin, houn'd wi' fear,
  Gaed like a glouf the bracken through,
Uncanny feet begoud tae steer,
  And cantrip din tae brew;

An awsome wecht o' nameless dreid
  Cam' like a mist attour my ken,
And aft I win't tae break this threid
  O' craft and breathe again;

Till, pile by pile, on howm and hill,
  The soughin' sprett took maik and tongue,
And in the gloamin' lown and shill
  This elfish lay was sung:—

" Alake ! alake ! sair weird tae dree
    Has he that wons the warlock's name ;
The licht o' life maun quat his ee,
    The look o' yird his frame.

" His heart maun shrivel like a threid
    That's held abune the ingle lowe,
And warplet roon' wi' en'less dreid
    His donart senses row.

" Men wat the land o' thocht is fair,
    And fain wad lichtly come and gang,
Yet reckna o' the waefu' care
    Oor ilka joy maun stang.

" Ne'er was a rose withoot a brier—
    The bonnier floo'r the faircer thorn—
For ilk guffaw some waefu' tear
    Maun fa' afore the morn.

"Then haud by what ye hae tae tyne—
    Haud weel by it, and want nae mair;
Ye'd aiblins rue fu' soothly syne
    Ye meddl't warlocks' ware."

STORM-STED.

'Twas twal o'clock—a gurly nicht—
    The shilpit mune rade high,
Deep-wadin' through a scoury brugh
    Wi' no a starnie by;
Atween and Wanlock hills the snaw
    Gade swirlin' by like stoure,
And like a spell its glamour fell
    Athort the mirksome muir.
A' efternune the feathery flecks
    Cam flichterin' through the air,
Wi' scarce a wauf o' win' tae drift
    The whiteness here nor there;
But or the blude reid sun had fa'n
    Aneth Glengaber's broo,

A norlan' blast begoud tae blaw
　　Wad chillt ye thro' and thro',
And as I barr't the ootmaist door,
　　And hapt me fiel and warm,
I maistly grat that ane I lo'ed
　　Micht still be in the storm.

But no—I kent that couldna be,
　　The wild sea sail was by,
My lang-lost lad was safe on shore,
　　His vessel high and dry.
Twa days at maist wad join the hearts
　　That Providence had spared
Tae pree a wee sowp o' the joy
　　That's wi' the lichtsome shared:
Twa wee short days—sune micht they slip!
　　A' days were lang tae me
That lay atween my langin' airms,
　　O Davy lad, and thee.

The day ne'er broke I didna miss
    Your fit beside the streams,
And ilka nicht wi' hungry lip
    I kist ye in my dreams.
But sune the weary oors wad pass
    That keepit us in pain,
And big wi' thocht o' comin' joy
    My heart bude greet again.

But wheesht! what waefu' cry was that
    Blawn in frae yont the hill,
When the wild storm had lown't a blink,
    And a' the glen was still?
It soundit like the eerie maen
    O' some half-waukent thing
Shot—or the dour blude at the heart
    Could nerve its brain tae spring;
A wild lost yaumer fleein' far
    Afore the sabbin' blast,

26   SCOTTISH POEMS.

And drappin' nameless dreid like dew
  On ilka thing it past.
Far i' the glen lichts fired at ance
  And heids cam oot tae hear
Gin neebors heard the waefu' cry
  That fillt theirsels wi' fear;
And ane by ane they ferlied there
  What that sad wail could be
That shook their hearts wi' tremblin
  As the tempest shakes the tree.

Again—my God! a human voice
  In agony and fear—
A human voice—it took nae skill
  The mournfu' truth tae hear.
Abune the roarin' o' the blast
  The voice cam lood and shill,
Some nichtit traveller, storm-sted,
  Was lairt ayont the hill.

Lichts sune were got, and bauld men oot,

    But a' their skill was vain;

They listent laigh and gleg, and socht

    By hill and stream and plain;

But never mair they heard the voice

    Had thrillt them tae the core,

And ane by ane they a' returned

    Forjeskit frae the muir.

And then we kent the ruthless snaw

    Had smoort him bye oor ken,

And there he'd lie until the Spring

    Had cleart the driftit glen.

The snaw lay lang that weary year,

    But lang afore it thow'd

I kent the name o' him that lay

    Aneth its spotless shroud:

Days past and Davy camena—days

    O' fearsome thocht tae me,

And ilka ane that broke I wist
　　Micht be the last I'd see:
I couldna bide in hoose or hauld,
　　But wandert far and near,
And prayt wi' a' my heart tae God
　　That Spring wad but appear,
That I micht see ance mair the lad
　　That thol't sae sair for me,
And lay him i' the mools where I
　　Hae howp sae sune to be:
The auld kirkyaird ayont the burn
　　Where e'enin' shadows fa',
And nicht is never rent in twain
　　Wi' voices through the snaw.

O God, that gart the tempest blaw
　　That wrocht sae muckle wae,
At the lown turnin' o' the nicht
　　I come ance mair tae pray.

Sair hast Thou strucken, but Thy wrath
   Wi' patient heart I bide,
And tae the chastenin' o' Thy rod
   I turn my waukit side.
This bonnie warld o' Thine has tint
   The licht that made it braw,
And fain wad I relinquish it
   For him that's noo awa'.

Tak' me but tae him or the snaw
   Brings back the thochts o' pain
That rise whene'er I see the hills
   In Winter's garb again;
Tak' me where nevermair the snaw
   'Ill smoor my comin' bliss,
And ither warlds maun yield the joy
   I never kent in this!

KATIE'S WELL.

[A small spring of crystalline purity in the lonely Pass
of Enterkin, well known to the natives of these parts, and
easily discovered by any strangers who may essay to climb
its rugged but not unlovely braes.]

O Katie, but thy lips are sweet!
    Their caller touch is life tae me,
As feckless in this mochy heat
    I bide a blink tae rest by thee.

Wow, but the braes are dour tae spiel;
    And what wi' loupin' hags and burns,
It's richt weel pleased I am tae kneel
    Beside thee till my breath returns.

And restin' here tae feel the calm
    O' this lown glen come owre my min',
While memory lea's me in a dwaum,
    Wi' gowden glints frae auld lang syne.

For Katie, I am muirlan' born
    And muirlan' bred juist like thysel',
And mony a time I've seen the morn
    Breck bonnie ower this lanesome fell.

And gin the gift o' speech were thine,
    It's mair than joyfu' I wad be
Tae streik me in the warm sunshine
    And niffer canny cracks wi' thee.

What wondrous tales I then micht hear,
    Tales that my heart is wae tae tyne,
O' fairies linkin' blithely here,
    And skirlin' in the clear muneshine!

What trysts o' lovers—ages deid—
  Were held aside this glistenin' stream,
Whase liquid wimplin' row'd a threid
  O' glamour through their thochtless dream!

What getherin's at the mirk o' nichts,
  When mune and sterns were smoort or dim,
And a' the misty muirlan' hichts
  Were quiverin' wi' the martyrs' hymn!

What cheeks, wi' different passions fired,
  Hae cule't them in thy crystal wave!
What hearts that reach'd thee wauf and tired
  Turn'd at thy simple magic brave!

Wha kens but Peden's haly lip,
  Or black M'Michael's bearded mou',
At times may hae been fain tae dip
  Where mine but gethert strength enow?

Or, sin' thy sweets are free as grace,
   E'en Clavers may hae lichtit doon,
Het frae some cantrip deevil's chase,
   And gledly quafft thy proffert boon!

Nae choice hast thou o' hynde or peer,
   Or gude or ill thou walest nane;
A' lips that thirst are welcome here,
   And free tae mak' thy walth their ain.

Herds on the hills, sin' time was young,
   Hae shared their mid-day meals wi' thee,
And mixed the music o' their tongue
   Wi' thy laich croon and en'less glee.

Nor art thou kind tae man alane,
   For ither voices lilt thy praise,
And ither tongues as blythe's my ain
   Aye roose ye tae the listenin' braes.

C

For scores o' lambs hae left the hill
  The freshness o' thy stream tae share;
And coontless birds hae drunk their fill,
  And still there's rowth for mony mair.

O winsome well that rins sae clear
  In this far-hid, unheard-o' glen!
'Twas Heaven alane that prankt thee here,
  Sic gift nae ither han' could sen'.

And while the mither hill hauds gude
  Thy siller spring may still be seen;
A wee fresh drap o' the very blude
  That keeps the heart o' the warld green!

THE HINMAIST CRICHTON.

Crichton o' Sanquhar had guid braid lan's,
And the feck o' the kintra-side in his han's;
Frae the brig o' Glenairlie tae Corsincon
There wasna a neuk that he didna own;
Baith couthie farm toon and herd's lane biel'
Rentit their hauld frae the Laird o' the Peel.

His credit was guid, and his pay nae waur,
His gien word reckont on near and far;
Nithsdale kentna the man e'er trowed
A differ in Crichton's word frae his gowd;
But were it a merk or a boddle broon,
The siller was there when the day cam' roon.

Fu' gleg i' the uptak' tae was he,

And a cout's best price at a glisk could see,

Whether he bocht for himsel', or saw

That knaves owrerax'd na the limit o' law;

At market or fair for a settlin' voice,

Crichton o' Sanquhar was a' men's choice.

And mair than that—he was held the pride

O' the women folk in the hale Nithside;

Kind tae the eild he had been a' his life,

And blithe could he crack wi' the douce gude-
    wife;

And the younglin' jauds, were they never sae shy,

Aye buskit their best when the Laird gaed by.

For Crichton o' Sanquhar was sax fit three,

Straucht as a sprout o' the forest tree,

Buirdly and stieve, o' a manly make,

Less like the esh than the lordly aik;

Firm on his fit, and free in his air,
And the gait o' his gangin' was leesome fair.

In trowth ye wad socht frae the craigs o' Scaur
Tae the laichmaist biel' on the braes o' Daer
Afore ye'd forgether wi' ane like him,
Sae leal in the heart, sae clean in the limb;
Few were his marrows, and fewer if e'er
His betters were kent, for they badena here.

But the bonniest day that the sun e'er saw
May be gurly and snell or the licht gae wa';
And afore his day was amaist began
The Laird o' the Peel was an alter'd man;
Dowie and dazed wi' a sair heid-hing,
Mair like a doyte than a mortal thing.

And a' folk ferlied—for nane could see
The gruesome weird that he had tae dree;

Hairst ne'er failed him, craps were gude,

As heich as the Cruffel the auld name stude;

At tryst or at market he still bure the bell,

And Crichton was Crichton tae a' but himsel'.

But weel I wat there was ane that kent

Hoo the runkles grew on a bree sae brent;

Her glamour had warplet the clear gaun
  brain.

And wastit his life wi' a cureless pain,

This curse gang wi' her wherever she be—

May she moop ill-mated, and barren dee!

Nane o' oor Nithsdale kimmers was she

That airtit the laird sae far ajee;

For though he was kind tae them, ilka yin,

And treatit them a' as he wad his kin,

Yet thocht he aye o' his ain degree,

And their honour was dear in his blameless ee.

But a loesome dame frae the border side

He had thocht fu' fain tae hae made his bride;

Sae wily and slee her lures she laid,

Sae keen wi' her noble victim play'd,

That he, wha ettlet her a' his ain,

Was seldom fasht wi' the lover's pain.

But oh, when he spiert her for her han',

Vowin' he'd mak' her the pride o' the lan',

Guess ye hoo siccan as him could thole,

Wi' the touchy pride o' his moorlan' soul,

When she leuch as merry as blithe could be,

And tauld him—it wisna her ain tae gie?

Frae that time forrit the laird was dune,

Fey as a nateral aneth the mune;

He daunert and drave for a while, nae doot,

But his cracks were sma', though he snooved
  aboot;

And a' folk kent, if they likit tae speak,

That Crichton's tether was ner the streik.

Aweel, ae mornin' the cry got up

The laird had gi'en Sanquhar and a' the slip.

The wuds were trackit, the moorlan's scoor'd,

The deepest wiels o' the Nith explored;

But trace o' the Crichton fand they nane—

And he never was seen in the kintra again.

This was the hinmaist o' that bauld line

That keepit the causey's croon lang syne—

A line in it's kintra's memory bricht

En't like a knotless threid i' the nicht,

And a heart nae man ever maistert yet

Dwined tae its deid at a woman's fit.

Ye wha hae love tae gie, look weel

That ye rest your wish wi' a bosom leal;

Braw braid acres and manly pairts

May dree nocht better than broken hearts,

And a wearifu' blank i' the warl' he'll pruve

That's matcht wi' a lady licht o' love.

THE WHAUP.

Fu' sweet is the lilt o' the laverock
    Frae the rim o' the clud at morn;
The merle pipes weel in his mid-day biel',
    In the heart o' the bendin' thorn;
The blithe, bauld sang o' the mavis
    Rings clear in the gloamin' shaw:
But the whaup's wild cry in the gurly sky
    O' the moorlan' dings them a'.

For what's in the lilt o' the laverock
    Tae touch ocht mair than the ear?
The merle's lown craik in the tangled brake
    Can start nae memories dear;

And even the sang o' the mavis

    But waukens a love-dream tame

Tae the whaup's wild cry on the breeze blawn

        by,

    Like a wanderin' word frae hame.

What thochts o' the lang gray moorlan'

    Start up when I hear that cry!

The times we lay on the heathery brae

    At the well, lang syne gane dry;

And aye as we spak' o' the ferlies

    That happen'd afore-time there,

The whaup's lane cry on the win' cam' by

    Like a wild thing tint in the air.

And though I ha'e seen mair ferlies

    Than grew in the fancy then,

And the gowden gleam o' the boyish dream

    Has slipp'd frae my soberer brain,

Yet—even yet—if I wander

   Alane by the moorlan' hill,

That queer wild cry frae the gurly sky

   Can tirl my heart-strings still.

FORGOTTEN.

O blessings on thy bonnie face,
   My winsome Mary Lee!
And lang may fickle fortune trace
   A flowery path for thee.
May joy bring dimples roon thy mouth,
   Through a' the gowden years,
And never drink be near his drouth
   That weets thy cheek wi' tears!

I hae been fain tae win the smile
   That waukent in thine een,
And wrocht wi' mony a tentie wile
   Tae please thee morn and e'en;

And though I didna daur to speak,
  My heart ne'er owned the fear
That thy young love wad ever seek
  Anither joe to cheer.

But now they say thou'rt woo'd and
    won,
  My winsome Mary Lee!
They tell me thou art woo'd and won,
  Withoot a thocht o' me;
Withoot a memory o' the days
  My heart will never tyne,
When thou and I amang the braes
  Gaed linkin' blithe lang syne.

O Mary, could thy heart forget
  The kiss it yielded coy,
That nicht beside the plantin' yett,
  When I was gyte wi' joy?

Could it forget? or did it ken
    That mine thrill'd thro' and thro'?
Thou should hae kept thy favours then,
    Or no' withheld them noo!

That nicht I vowed a solemn aith,
    My winsome Mary Lee,
That nocht wad shake the simple faith
    I had in love and thee:
I pledged my soul upon the spot,
    Whatever fate micht fa';
But thou that gied, as sune forgot,
    And never lo'ed ava!

And still I dinna curse the day,
    When first thy face was seen;
Though thou hast left me wauf and
      wae,
    I'm glad that day has been.

In memory's casket where each gem
  O' happiness is stored,
Nae days will ever match wi' them
  When thou wert maist adored.

Fareweel! may gladness be thy lot,
  Without a grief to mar;
A lanely wanderer clean forgot,
  I bless thee from afar:
And may thy lover ne'er hae cause
  A dule like mine tae dree—
Fareweel, I canna ca' thee fause!
  Forgetfu' Mary Lee!

NECONY.

Roun' by Necony the heather blumes bonnie,

    And sweet is the lilt o' the mosscheiper's sang;

But though y'd gang farrer and no fin ocht fairer,

    Yet roun' by Necony I carena tae gang:

I'll rove by Petrennock, Snarswater or Mennock,

    The stey craigs o' Carron I'll still spiel wi' glee;

But roun' by Necony there's something no canny,

    And he that's no fley'd for't is baulder than me!

I canna tell whether the blume o' the heather

    Be reider owre yonder than heather suld be,

But aye when I see it in blossom, tae me it

    Taks shape like the dreepin o' blude in the ee:

D

The mosscheiper's liltin', at ither times meltin',

    Gangs thro' the daz'd heart wi' a dirl and a stoun;

In yaumers sae eerie, wi' naething else near ye,

    Ye grue as a warlock were raisin' the soon.

But gruin or glowrin', nocht mair overpow'rin'

    Will stertle the calm on the breist o' the glen;

Nae warlock or worricoo bides in Necony noo,

    Scarce can ye trace its connection wi' men:

But though they be rotten, their memory forgotten,

    And naething be kent o' their deeds or their doom,

God's mercy, Necony! there's something no canny

    Has happent tae cleed ye in glamour and gloom.

WINTER.

I canna thole the breeze that springs
    Ayont the wastlin' sea,
Its lown saft music only flings
    A dowie dwawm on me;
Far liefer wad I hear the blast
    Roar owre the norlan' main,
For winter's fury smoors the past,
    And lea's me man again.

In pleasure's lap I lay and slum'd
    The leelang simmer through,
Where nocht but weeds o' idless blum'd,
    And the whimprin' wast win' blew.

But like some moth, attour the slugh

    I lap at winter's ca',

And leuch tae hear his lanesome sugh

    Come thro' the driftin' snaw.

Then blaw thou blast, baith lood and snell,

    Thy breath but wauks my glee;

The reid blude risin' frank and fell,

    Comes dinlin' tae my bree.

And on the stey storm-blaudit hill

    Defying nicht and thee,

I gether mair o' wit and will

    Than simmer e'er could gie.

JILTED.

Lass, gin that winsome face o' thine
 Had been as dear's it micht tae me,
I wad been laith sae sune tae tyne
 By fair or fause its birkie glee;
And aiblins micht hae hirselt fain
 Tae airt its glints my gait again.

But though nae ither lass could steer
 My dour content while thou wert kin',
Ne'er trow that I sall lack for cheer
 Because thy smiles nae mair are mine—
For fish, they say, are soomin' yet
 As guid as ever bagg'd a net.

And I, wha thocht tae licht on ane—

    A diamen 'mang the mennin fry—

A'though begunk'd, may cast again,

    And fankle better still forbye;

And when the salmon's safe on shore,

    Lichtlie the grilse that slipt afore.

But this abune the lave I'll seek—

    A lassie modest, sweet, and kin',

For glintin' ee and glowin' cheek

    Gang aften wi' as toom a min';

An' I'll be waft nae mair ajee

    By a' the charms o' cheek or ee.

The lintie's cleed o' hodden grey

    Is no the spell that hauds him dear:

Wha cares if he be stour or gay

    As lang's his bonnie sang we hear?

Sae I'll let maik and feathers gang,

   And woo my lintie for her sang.

Gowks gather gear for loons tae wair,

   As thriftless as theirsel's were near;

And I was daft tae hoord my care

   For ane that snool't at sic-like gear;

But sin' I've tint baith it and thee,

   I'll bide contented tae be free.

MAY MORIL.

We wonn'd in a lanesume muirlan' glen—
    May Moril and me,
And little we kent o' the ways o' men—
    May Moril and me;
But if little we kent, far less did we care,
    Sae couthie and vaunty can true love be,
For we ettlet nae joy in the warld sae rare,
But micht ha'e been match'd in the muirlan' there,
When the glamour o' love fillt a' the air
    And we waded the brackens knee by knee.

Kings and their coorts micht founder or soom
    On their shiftin' sea;

But we wi' their fate ne'er fasht oor thoom—

      May Moril and me.

We kent that the warld wad trintle and turn

    Wi' mickle o' pleasure and mair o' wae,

Sae doun by the banks o' the wimplin' burn

We strayed i' the dawin o' love's sweet morn,

And we nippet the blossom and jinkt the thorn

    As the lang saft simmer row'd away.

The brier rose grew on the open shaw

      In the lown clear air,

And it and the milk-white blume o' the haw

      I twined in her hair;

And she sat on the brae like a gowd-croont queen

    And fliskit her sceptre o' birk wi' pride;

And I—I thocht that the joys we ken't

As lang as we socht them ne'er wad en't,

And e'en when oor hinmaist breath was spent

    We'd sleep i' the muirlan' side by side.

But alas! for the unkent weirds o' man
Are kittle tae dree,
And little we trow'd that oor gowden plan
Sae brittle wad be.
But the heaven aboon us nae doot saw
Our love was mair than it ocht tae be,
For we hadna been marriet a year and a day
When, sair forfeuchen, my winsome May
On the breist o' her dawtie dwined away,
And my heart-strings crack't when I saw her dee.

O hooly and wae I laid her doun
In her hinmaist rest,
And back i' the glen I lookit roun'
At oor herrit nest;
And bare, bare noo were the muirlan's grey,
Where the licht o' her love gart a' things shine,
And I saw that nocht i' the warld wad be
The same as it was tae my joyfu' ee

When we wadit the brackens knee by knee,

    And sweet May Moril was hale and mine.

The brier rose blumes on the open shaw,

      As it did langsyne,

And the milk-white blossom hings on the haw

      I' the warm sunshine.

But blossom and bud hae tint their charms,

    They may rot where they gether or fa' for me,

And O! gin I hadna a thocht tae rise

Tae sweet May Moril ayont the skies,

Where my heart baith e'enin' and mornin' lies,

    Hoo sad wad the lang grey muirlan' be!

THE COTTAR'S COMFORT.

It's no a brag tae threep that nane
 Roun' a' oor eident kintra side
Gang through their darg mair blythe and fain
 Than me, or wi' as tentie pride;
And yet at orra times the dour
 Dreich draidle dings me sair ajee,
And blin's my kennin' wi' a stour,
 Attour the whilk it downa see.

I ken that some maun moil, I ken
 It's this that gars the ba' gang roun';
Nor wad I quat that ither men
 Micht geck me for a menseless loon:

But whyles, for a' my wit, I trow,
 A cottar's cark is sair tae bide,
And aft wad rest my wearied pow
 Doon i' the mools, by Mary's side.

But aye, whenever hampert sae
 Wi' thochts that life is mirk and snell,
Ayont the gloamin' muir I gae
 A lanely dauner by mysel';
And in yon lown deep-rifted glen
 My wauf forjeskit fit wuns by,
And comfort, tint on warldly men,
 Slips canny in its room forbye.

For there, aneth the darklin' lift,
 Wi' God's ain glowin' een abune,
I min' ance mair the warplet drift
 O' things that daz'd me in the toon;

As ae wee stern gies little licht,

　　But cheerly blinks amang the lave,

Sae I maun haud me blythe and bricht

　　Till mornin' daws athort the wave.

LANGSYNE.

" What means Langsyne?" oor fremit comrade speir'd,

   Aboot the turn o' nicht when havers fail,

   And some ane hinted as we raise tae skail

Tae close wi' " Auld Langsyne:" sic joy appeared

In ilka face, sae kindly grew ilk tongue;

   And as the dear auld owrecome tirl'd atween

   Han' gruppit han' sae leal, and frae oor een

Tears fell sae fast—the lad was donart dung.

And though a' nicht his voice amang oor ain

   Had gart the reekit rafters ring wi' glee

   In that auld bield o' his ayont the sea,—

Yet when the Scottish hearts did loup fou fain

   Tae raise this chorus, little wit could see,

Be Scotsmen wha they micht, that he was nane.

"O bairn!" quo' I, "here in your ain dear hame
    Life snooves awa' sae cannily that ye
    Hae nocht tae grieve for, or wad wis' tae see
E'er altered,—sae langsyne is but a name
Tae you and yours; sma' differ wad it prove
    Gin ye were tynin' what ye hae tae fin'
    What ye hae had afore; but tae sic men
As sang e'enoo—langsyne is Scotland, luve,
And youth;—the land that saw them blythe as you;
    The lichtsome heart that they maun ken nae mair,
    The leal bauld bairntime, free o' cark and care.
Sic sweets as thae, and mony mair I troo—
The wale o' life's few pleasures—ye maun tyne
Afore ye dree the weird o' 'Auld Langsyne.'"

MY AIN HILLS.

The bonnie hills o' Wanlock,
 I've spielt them ane and a',
Baith laich and heich and stey and dreich,
 In rain and rowk and snaw:
And owre a' ither mountains
 Nane else e'er bure the gree;
Nae peaks that rise aneth the skies
 Can raise sic thochts in me.

I've warslet up Ben Lomond
 When simmer deckt its side,
And grey Goatfell, that stan's itsel'
 In solitary pride;

E

But frae their wildest grandeur
   Wi' sma' concern I'd turn
Tae ae wee glen, wi' some I ken,
   By Wanlock's wimplin' burn.

For there wi' chiels far 'sunder'd,
   I roved in glee lang syne,
And never fit was lichter yet
   Amang the muirs than mine;
And wi' sic shouts o' gladness
   We startlet hill and plain,—
I'd tyne a year o' a' things here
   Tae raise the like again.

But we are lads nae langer,
   And time is gowd they say;
The hills sae green are seldom
     seen
   When ance we start tae stray;

And mair than time is wantin',
　　For gin we a' were there,—
Wha kens? the min' micht no incline
　　Its former sports tae share.

O, bonnie hills o' Wanlock!
　　What　pranks　auld　Time　does
　　　　play?
I kent nae change in a' your range
　　When I cam' here the day:
But faces that I met wi'
　　Are surely altert sair;
And some I ken hae left the glen
　　We'll never meet wi' mair.

But though the fit may wander,
　　The heart can aye be true,
And mony a yin, I brawly ken,
　　Wad fain be here e'enoo;

And mony a weary comrade

Like me fu' aften prays,

That the bonnie hills o' Wanlock

May see his hinmaist days.

AMANG THE BRUME.

Doon amang the brume, in yon dowie glen yestreen,
    I heard a safter melody than mavis ever sang;
And I couldna fen' but listen tho' a mist cam' in my een,
    And ilka word gaed through me like a stang—
"O bonnie rides the boat when the simmer win' is lown,
    And the gowden lift abune her is nae sooner than
        the sea;
But when the win' is waken't, and the wave has gurly
        grown,
What troubles maun the weary boatie dree!"

Doon amang the brume, when the eerie wail gaed by,
    A dwawm cam' owre my kennin', and I saw a boat
        gaun doon;

And I wist the warst had happen'd, for I heard a
waefu' cry,

And again the voice gaed through me wi' a stoun—

" O! bonnie is the lift when the storm has cleart the
blue,

And bonnie is the water when it settles braid and
fair;

But the bonnie face o' somebody will smile nae mair
on you,

His boat will ride the waters nevermair."

HAME'S AYE HAME.

(THE LINTIE'S DEFENCE OF THE MOORLAND.)

" Bonnie wee bird wi' the blithesome ee,
 Happin' aboot on the bare hillside,
Liltin' yer sang wi' a heart as free
 As the breeze that scatters it far and wide.
What can hae ta'en ye—if I may spier—
That ye suld bide i' the muirlan' here?"

" What can hae ta'en me? Whaur wad I gang
 Tae look for a joy I lack e'enoo?
Is there a spot thir hills amang
 Wi' heather as bonnie or lift as blue?
Tell me the marrow o' Arthur's Grain,
This lane lown corrie I ca' my ain."

" Arthur's Grain is but scraggy and bare,
　　Hardly a bracken tae bield ye here;
Mennock has wudlan's bonnie and fair
　Whaur ye micht shelter the leelang year,
And join wi' the lave o' the feather'd thrang,
Deavin' the wuds wi' yer joyfu' sang."

" Mennock is bonnie, and fair, and fine,
　　But mony a blither than me is there:
And wha wad listen tae sangs like mine
　　When the wuds are ringin' wi' soons sae
　　　rare?
On the bleak, bare muir, or the misty glen
Ye bless the voice ye wad ne'er hear then."

" But gleds come whiskin' athort the muir,
　　Yer wee heart loups tae yer neb wi' dreid;
Ye ken thae brackens are no secure,
　　Ilk wauf o' the win' micht shaw yer heid;

And what wad become o' yer artless glee
Gin ye catcht the tail o' his ruthless ee?"

"The gleds come roun' by the muir as ye say,
　　And oh, but their glance is gleg and keen;
But better a gled in the open day
　　Than a hoolit's skraich i' the mirksome e'en;
When the heart's warm bluid begins tae creep
Wi' an eerie chill, and ye daurna sleep."

"But think o' the storms ye maun endure,
　　And the faucht ye hae for a pyke betimes.
It's hard, dry fare on a barren muir,
　　And little ye get for yer winsome rhymes;
And sangs come best frae a singer's heid
That ne'er maun think on claes or breid."

"Storms at the warst maun e'en blaw by,
　　And the young ling blumes are sweet tae pree;

And then sae fair is the simmer sky
   Ye'd sing for pleasure as weel as me.
Claes, I'll be thankfu', come aff haun,
   And a gey wee mouthfu' keeps me gaun."

" Aweel, wee bird, I hae said my say,
   Ye may bide i' the cauld, bare muir for me;
Ne'er think I'd be fain tae see ye away,
   'Twas a' for yersel' I made sae free.
The muir wad be dowie and deid I troo
Gin it hadna a leevin' voice in you."

" Nae mair; gin the voice o' the muir be sweet,
   Still let it be as it aye has been;
In simmer or winter, cauld or weet,
   The hills are dear to my constant een;
For wi' birds as wi' mair things I could name
Nae maitter hoo lowly—hame's aye hame."

SOMETHING WRANG.

I.

Saft is the note o' the roguish bird that sits in the
flowery thorn,
When he woos some jaud frae the neebor shaw tae
lie a' nicht at his side;
Blithe is the blink o' his gleg wee ee when it opes in
the mirk o' the morn,
And sees the dear thing cuddlet sae close he canna
but chirrup for pride.
But never did lovesick bird on the bough e'er pipe sae
sweet for a mate,
Never sic joy in a feathered breast has been sin' the
warld begun,

As I saw unseen when my winsome wife cam' oot tae
    the door and flate,
  That Willie suld leave her a day for the waters,
    Willie, her favourite son.

II.

" Gie me your rod," quo she, " and bide ye at hame,
    I hae muckle tae say;
  Ye come like a glouf o' the winter sun, yin hardly
    kens ye are here,
Till the wee short fortnicht has worn tae an end, and
    then ye're aff and away;
  And we seena the glisk o' your bonnie face mabye
    for anither year;
Forbye ye ken o' the tryst I made wi' the neebors up
    by in the glen,
  That sax in the e'enin' wad bring them your faither,
    and me, and yoursel';

It never wad dae tae begunk them noo, especial, for
weel ye maun ken,
That the wish o' my heart and your faither's is bent
on your matin wi' Nell.

III.

" She's a trig lass Nell, and a bonnie, her marrows are
no tae be fun'
For parishes roun' though mony are in them bonnie
and braw!
At this the rogue leuch till I thocht he wad fa'n tae
the grun',
And cryin' oot, ' Mither, that's gospel,' he hirselt
aboot tae gae wa';
She, shakin' her nieve at the laddie, ance mair bade
him think on the time,
And then stood watchin' his buirdly make as he
snoov'd in the dawin' alang,

Till he cam' tae the neuk where the fitroad dips, and
    he took tae the heather tae climb,
When he turnt for a moment and shouted, ' I'll be,
    if there's naething gaes wrang.'"

IV.

Back tae the cottage she turnt her aboot, wi' the licht
    o' her love in her ee,
And I met her fair i' the teeth and speir'd gin the
    tryst she made wad be held;
And she, yet warm wi' her darlin's words, in simple
    and mitherly glee,
Gade by wi' an answer that left me wauf, like a
    staggerin' stirk half-fell'd;
For whether it was that the voice unkent had some-
    thing o' dreid in itsel',
Or whether my heart got a haud o' the words, like
    the owrecome o' some auld sang,

I never took tent, but an awsome chill on the heat o'
    my heart-strings fell,
    And I shook like a three days' bairn when she said,
        " He'll be, if there's naething gaes wrang."

v.

" If there's naething gaes wrang," quo' I tae mysel ten
    times in the coorse of the day,
    What nonsense is this I'm wastin' my heart tae
        cherish sae constant and keen?
I'm certain that nocht can gae wrang wi' the lad, let
    him rove where he may,
    Aneth the blue dome o' the lift, in the howe o' the
        mountains sae green;
But aft as I banished the gruesome thocht that follow'd
    the words like a shade,
    As aften the feelin' cam' till me unsocht, and
        wrocht on my mind like a spell,

Till substance could beir it na langer, and quatin' my
    darg at the spade,
And sayin', " I'm gaun tae meet Willie," I made for
    the road tae the hill.

VI.

A dour black clud owre the wedderglim darkent the
    lift and the glen,
    I kent it had shapit for something like this for
        nearly a fortnicht gane by,
But thocht it wad keepit a day or twa mair, else
    Willie wad need made a fen',
    Tae bide at the cottage contentit, and haud himsel'
        cosie and dry;
For though it be nocht for a shepherd like me to be
    oot in the weet or the storm,
    Wi' never a bield frae the angry blash, but the bouk
        o' an auld grey cairn;

Thae whitefaced toon's fowk gree far best wi' the air
    weel tempert and warm,
And needs maun look after their tender hides like a
    shilpit lass or a bairn.

VII.

And weel did it heppen for me that day I carena'd for
    weather or win',
    For juist as I managed the Wingate brae-heid the
        black clud broke wi' a roar,
And a' doon Daur tae the Hass o' Benuff, wi' an
    uncolike deafenin' din;
    The claps o' the thunner seem'd chasin' ilk ither
        like waves on a storm-lasht shore;
And oot o' the mids' o' the collied lift richt doon on
    the howe o' Petrail,
    The reid jagg'd bolts o' the fireflaucht flichtert and
        skirr'd alang,

F

And a lownness deeper than ocht but death had fa'n on
the mirksome dale,

Afore the big draps cam' tae the grun', and I thocht
on the something gaun wrang.

VIII.

" The Lord look efter my storm-sted lad, and haud
him a wee in Thy care!"

My heart broke oot wi' the wilyart cry, as I saw, far
doon in the glen,

A something that lookt like the shape o' a man come
owre frae the dazzlet muir,

And crossin' Petrail at the Peden burnfit, come on
tae the hill at a sten';

I kent it was nane but the laddie I socht, in pairt by
his lassie-like gang,

As far frae the lamp o' the muirlan' herd as the mirk
is far frae the mune;

And I thocht tae mysel', "Thank God for His care,
 he's safe, and there's naething gane wrang,
And Jean'll be prood o' us baith this nicht, let oor
 comin' be syne or sune."

IX.

But juist as the gled words loupt tae my lip a flash
 like a furnace gade by,
And I trow'd that the lift wad be riven in bits by
 the horrible crack owreheid,
And the bolt o' the levin had whizzed sae close it left
 me birselt and dry,
And the din o' the thunner had dung me sae I
 stood for the moment deid;
And the first wild look I gat at the howm where
 Willie had ta'en tae the hill,
The turf had been plewt wi' a fiery cou'ter deep as
 a drain in spring;

And oot in the saft green hollow ḥis corpse was
    streekit stiffly and still,
  And a' that was left o' my bonnie bairn was a
    blackent and gruesome thing.

x.

God o' the thunner! forgie me the aith that stertled
    the hills o' my hame,
  When I saw Thy creature, the pride o' my life,
    struck doon i' that fearsome day;
I coo'r at the fit o' Thy gowden throne, and own wi' a
    heart o' shame,
  That my spirit gade up in a desperate word, mak's
    mortal rebellious tae say:
But Thou kens only—as ken Thou maun—that mair
    than my ain wild wae,
  I thocht on the mither that sat by the ingle wi' heid
    boo't forrit tae hear

The fit that wad nevermair lichten her look as she
heard it climbin' the brae,
The voice that mair than a lover's vows had charms
for her eager ear.

XI.

Thou kens, O Lord! what treasure was set on the
young life nippet sae sune,
Thou kens hoo bitter a weird Thy will has laid on
us baith tae dree,
And Lord! Thou kens Thy servant's heart ne'er carps
that Thy will be dune,
Though the daein' o't whiles brings little but wae
on mine as weel as on me:
And e'en as the knowledge o' a' that is can never be
tint tae Thy sicht,
And Thy strong richt airm that is swift tae strike is
aften as swift tae save.

I bide in the faith that ae black blot 'll fade in the
    bleezin' licht
That gies me a look o' my bonnie bairn on the
    tither side o' the grave.

XII.

I seldom can think on the wearifu' past—I maistly
    leeve in a dwawm;
The ills o' the warl are little tae thole when the first
    sair bruilzie is bye,
And the terrible sicht, that day in the glen, has left me
    donart and calm,
Sae calm that aften I ferlie sair gin the springs o' my
    passion be dry,
For even when Jeanie, my winsome wife, had follow'd
    her son to the grave,
The never a tear-drap saftened my cheek, but aye
    like an auld auld sang

That weird ghaist murmur grew in my heart as dour
as the sough o' the wave,

And I ken that the best o' my life had en't when I
grued at the " something wrang."

DECEIVED.

Lie still my loupin' heart,
  And dinna fash sae sair,
For lover's joy or smart
  Can come to you nae mair;
Wae worth the hapless day
  That e'er ye kent the same,
Sin' I am leifu' forced to say
  Man's love is but a name!

Ae simmer scarce has flown
  Sin' I was jimp and sma',
But noo my last year's gown
  It downa meet ava :

My cheek is wat wi' tears,
   Frae wells that winna dry;
And a' my heart is torn wi' fears,
   And a' my peace is by.

O thochtless lips that tauld
   The joys ye couldna hide,
When Robin, blythe and bauld,
   Was constant at your side.
What madness urged ye then,
   Wi' ready glee, tae say
The weary truth nae man suld ken
   But after mony a nay.

For man suld crave his joy,
   And woman suld deny;
But whatna maid is coy
   When life and love are high.

The a' I had to gie,
   I gied it frank and fair,
And noo my wretched heart maun dree
   The dule for evermair.

The spring may airt the leaf
   Tae cleed the naked tree,
But nocht can hide the grief
   Forever bare in me.
Nocht but the weird o' death,
   That's settlin' owre the glen,
Can richt a lover's wrangèd aith,
   Or bring me joy again.

O lasses, rosy, rare,
   That ettle love sae sweet,
I red ye weel tak' care
   What fitroad wins your feet;

The richt ane may be fair,—

   But gin ye try the wrang,

Ye'll fin' a' pleasures tasted there

   En's wi' an ethert's stang.

A SPRIG O' HEATHER.

I.

It cam' in the faulds o' a lovenote true—
    This sprig o' heather,
Straucht doon frae the mountains whaur it grew
    In the warm spring weather;
Fresh, wi' the fresh wild air o' the glens,
Dear, frae the dear young thing that kens
Hoo fain my wearifu' heart wad be
Tae bide wi' her ain on the muirland lea,
    Amang the heather.

II.

It brings me a glisk o' the hichts and howes
    Whaur grey mists gether,

Whaur blithe birds sing and the wee burn rows
  In the wilds o' heather;
The scent o' the sweet thing fills my min'
Like the croon o' an auld sang kent langsyne,
And my heart gangs back to the joyfu' days,
When its beat was licht as the breeze that strays
  Amang the heather.

III.

O bonniest gem o' the treeless wild!
  I carena whether,
As neither a flow'r nor a tree thou'rt styled,—
  Thou art dear as either:
And lang as the linty bigs her nest
In the bield o' thee on the mountain crest,
Sae lang will the muirlan' heart o' me
Hae a nameless joy it can only pree
  Amang the heather.

IV.

The lily sae mim or the blude-reid rose
May charm anither,
But a Scotsman's heart in his bosom glows
At the sicht o' heather;
Whether it wave on the breezy hills,
And a' the air wi' its fragrance fills,
Or comes as a token that some sweet face
Is missin' his ain at the trystin' place
Amang the heather.

V.

And oh, tae hae haud o' that face e'enoo!
Row'd close thegither,
Where nocht but the sun e'er dichts the dew
Frae the wavin' heather;
Row'd close thegither aneth ae plaid

When lichts were gloamin' and winds were laid;

And never a tongue but the bird's abune

Could speak o' the ferlies said or dune

      Amang the heather!

ENGLISH POEMS.

THE SPIRIT OF THE MOOR.

MORTAL.

Whither so fast, fair wilding of the mountain?
 'Tis late for such as thou to wander here,
Unguarded, by the lonely wizard fountain
 That bubbles in the moonlight cool and clear:
This is no place to tryst with ardent lover,
 And listen vows, enraptured though they be;
A sweeter spot would thoughtful love discover

 To pass the mellow gloaming hour with thee.
Hath night enwrapt thy maiden soul in glamour,
 That thou shouldst linger here beneath the moon,
Where plovers' wail and curlews' ceaseless clamour
 Do mar the solemn midnight's soothing boon?

If so—a kindred spell hath surely won me
  To gaze upon thy beauteous form, that seems,
With the pale moonbeam raining glory on thee,
  Th' inspiring muse of my poetic dreams.
Were not the days of faery dead for ever
  I'd look for elfin vassals by thy side,
For ne'er on heath or holt, by wood or river,
  Have I beheld such comeliness and pride.
Bright eyes that thrill my being with their
    brightness,
  Long locks that flutter freely in the wind,
A foot whose firmest step is airy lightness,—
  All speak a spirit bountiful and kind:
Then, if as frank as thou art fair of feature,
  One kiss—I ask it here on bended knee—
The pass-word of a kindly common nature,
  A bond of mortal faith 'tween thee and me!
We meet upon the mountain wild and lonely
  That never met before on hill or plain,

Thou fair—I fearless—grant me this, this only,

    One little kiss and then we part again!

SPIRIT.

We meet upon the mountain wild and lonely

    That never met before on hill or plain;

Yet think not that we meet to part, and only

    This kiss shall be for aye between us twain.

Beneath these stars that stud the vault of heaven

    Long have I sought a soul to mate with mine;

At length unto my weary search is given

    The bliss that makes mortality divine.

Is it not writ in answer to my prayer

    " The first whose voice ye listen is your lord;

Shun him that fears, he is a false betrayer,

    But take the dauntless mortal at his word."

Men come and go upon this lonely mountain,

    I meet them in the silence and the gloom;

But one by one they turn them from the fountain,

   And I am left alone to wail my doom:

These eyes that strike within and heat thy being

   Have terrors for thy mates of lesser mould;

The earthy drags who turn about and fleeing

   Go back into their trammels and their gold;

Who could not nerve their courage to the stature

   That shrinks not in the company of gods,

But crippled from the partial hand of nature

   Break into dust at death like parchéd clods.

But thou, in manly guise and godly spirit,

   Far other future looms ahead for thee;

A nameless dower of bliss thou shalt inherit

   Shower'd down upon the barren moor by me.

Yet shrink not—I am little more than mortal,

   Press that soft hand, or kiss that softer brow;

Thy faltering soul is at Elysium's portal,

   Say will it muster heart and enter now?

MORTAL.

A spell is on me, viewless bands enthrall me,
  The grosser world is passing from my ken;
In the far ether fairy voices call me,
  Ethereal music thrills the lonely glen:
Sweet maid, I can but stand apart and wonder,
  I know not what to think of this or thee;
Some charm hath rent forbidden things in
    sunder,
  Or touched the iris of my sight to see.
A little while—and this bare stretch of mountain
  Was cold beneath the moon's unwarming ray,
And, as I thought, beside the wizard fountain
  Two mortals met upon a lonely way.
The beauty of the one had nerved the other
  To crave the favour of affection's boon—
The chaste kiss of a sister to a brother,
  Given by the sanction of the maiden moon.

But now the mist that dimm'd my gaze is lifted,

    I see thee in thy weirdly robes arrayed,

With beauty wild and wondrous glamour gifted,

    The living semblance of a fairy maid.

I see thee thus: I who can show no token

    That earthly love will evermore be mine;

The tie that binds me to the world is broken,

    I feel in spirit I am only thine.

I bow before the eyes that so enthrall me,

    I yield thee all the future I can claim;

Tell me, sweet lady, what my tongue may call thee,

    That on my heart it may impress thy name.

SPIRIT.

I gently pass among the whispering bracken

    That toss their tresses in the morning wind;

I float along the curlew's call, and waken

    An echo of it in thy musing mind:

I touch thee in the breeze that sweeps the mountain,

    I kiss thee in the mist that clasps the glen,

I murmur to thee in the lonely fountain

    That bubbles in the wild, remote from men.

There is no sight or sound in all the many

    That long have led thee to these lonely ways,

Whether thy fancy rove through hollows fenny

    Or seek the sunshine of the upper braes—

But doth the charm that thrills thy kindred spirit

    And holds its silent worship firm and sure,

In all its weird variety inherit

    From me, the spirit of the lonely moor.

Long have I watched the simple fondness growing

    That shows the flower of love now owned by

        thee,

While I unseen the chosen seeds was sowing,

    Whose blossom bourgeons out so fair to see.

And never yet hath mortal maid enchanted

    Her chosen champion with bliss so rare,

As to the heart of him is freely granted
  Who lives the spirit's moorland life to share.
I'll still be with thee quickening into motion,
  The tides of song that leap in light and glee;
Enough if, answering to my warm devotion,
  The murmur of these tides doth breathe of me.

THE CAIRN ON THE HILL.

Among the Lowther hills there is a grave,—

A cairn rough-shapen on the moorland lea—

And many a fond attempt I made to learn

To whose remains that mound a shelter gave,

And what of pride or strength might buried be,

Under the guardianship of such a cairn;

But to no useful end,—it was a mystery

Unveiléd in traditionary lore,

Passed over in the careless page of history,

Forgotten 'mong the glorious songs of yore;

Yet on the fragrant heath I've often lain,

When the lone plover and the wild curlew

Startled the moorland with their mournful screams;

Or, while the brooding gloom that wrapt the plain

Upon my soul its speechless glamour threw,
Sat pensively, and crooned my gloaming dreams.

I.

O thou in whom death's peaceful slumber
  Hath wrought the calm earth doth not know,
  Round whom no more the wave shall flow,
That wearies with its constant cumber
  All hearts that climb the climbing tide;
  What perfect rest it is that comes,
  Unsought, and all life's ache benumbs,
  Here where the wander'd wild-bee bums
  Along the mountain side.

II.

Not in the far heart of the city
  Broods such a silence as is here;
  There sculptur'd towers and tombs appear,

To nourish love or waken pity
>   With memories of the dust below;
>   Forgetfulness of life is here,
>   The very Lethe of the bier,
>   And all along the moorland drear
>   The dreary sense doth grow.

III.

Meet resting-place it is, though lonely,
>   For mortal dead to name and fame;
>   And sure thine outlaw'd bones can claim
No righting at our hands, but only
>   To lie where they have lain so long.
>   If song or legend rung with praise
>   Of thee, thine ashes we might raise,
>   And honour yet; but blame or praise
>   Of thee is not in song.

IV.

The mountain peaks are bare and hoary

That sentinel thy lonely grave;

No tree doth spring, no branches wave

To catch the burden of the story

The breeze brings up the slumbering glen;

And with its woful tale untold

The wind goes o'er the silent wold,

And all the secrets it doth hold

Are lost to mortal ken.

V.

Perchance if on this naked mountain

Some pine had stretch'd its arms abroad,

And hawk or raven made abode

Within its crest above the fountain

That flows unshaded as we see,

At night the harping wind had stay'd

Amongst its boughs, and music made,

And to some gifted bard betray'd
    The secrets hid with thee.

VI.

But naught is known—the purple heather
    Is speechless in thy blame or praise ;
    The mourners who of old did raise
This cairn grown grey in wind and weather,
    Say neither thou wert base or brave,
    Conjecture—rumour—all are mute,
    Tradition—legend—know thee not,
    These stones that mark the lonely spot
    But say—it is a grave.

VII.

Yet do I yearn to know thy station !
    Perhaps upon the scroll of fame
    Some kindly hand has traced thy name

A warrior in the Scottish nation

    Whose actions show'd thee good and brave;

    If so—'tis meet that thou shouldst sleep,

    Among these mountains stern and steep

    That saw thy fatal broadsword sweep

      Tyrants to a bloody grave.

VIII.

Perhaps thy lot was but the tending

    Of fleecy flocks upon these hills,

    Where the grey heath and noisy rills

Beneath a maze of mist are blending

    Their features in the autumn gloam ;

    Here while the summer hours flew by,

    Wrapt in thy chequered plaid to lie,

    And watch the clouds across the sky

      Float on, like flakes of foam

IX.

Or—higher thought—who knows but under
　　These bleached stones the dust may rest
　　That once was in the van to breast
The wave that dash'd itself in thunder
　　Against the rock of Scotland's faith?
　　A martyr falling, book in hand,
　　When that rapacious Highland band
　　O'erran the vext unhappy land,
　　And doom'd the good to death.

X.

Whate'er thou wert, forgotten sleeper,
　　Will alter not thy deep repose;
　　Oblivion hides thy joys and woes,
And does not own a cavern deeper
　　Than shrouds thy life from light and me;

H

For mists and mankind come and go,

Midnight shapes flit to and fro,

And, thinking not—unthought of—throw

Shadows o'er thy grave and thee.

XI.

This is the meed the earth doth render

To all except her brightest names;

A little while their merit claims

Her pride, that cherish and defend her,

And then they're lost or toss'd away;

'Tis surely lesson this to me,

From quest of earthly fame to flee,

And rest my wishes where they'll be

A treasure trove for aye.

HERE AND HEREAFTER.

In the utmost limits of time,
    On the verge of the great To Be,
The sunny cliffs of a beauteous clime
    Hang over a stormy sea;

And darkness broods on the deep,
    Though the land-lights far away
Are seen sometimes from the barks that creep
    On that perilous ocean way;

And a voice cries from the shore
    To guide the mariners home,
But often 'tis drown'd by the breakers' roar
    And the hiss of the blinding foam.

For many a bark goes down,

And many a soul is slain ;

But scarce has the spirit to darkness flown

When the billow gapes again.

And the air is filled with wail,

And curses, and cries of fear,

And the shrieking of spirits in sore travail

For a help that is not near.

The heart must be fearless and brave,

And deaf to the tempest's roar,

That could steer thro' the strength of the rushing wave

And land on the distant shore;

For the path is girt with dread,

And set with the snares of sin,

And the monsters that crowd the deep are fed

With what the wild wave sucks in.

There Pleasure spreads her lures,

   And watches with eager eyes

Till the tangled mesh of her net secures

   The soul of her thoughtless prize.

There Mammon is busy, too,

   With whispers of power untold;

And the bright cheek loses its radiant hue

   In its greed for the yellow gold.

And the mirage, Ambition, shows

   The glittering baubles of fame,

And tosses a withering laurel to those

   Who waste their lives for a name.

Naught that is there doth last—

   For scarce has the goal been won

When Death with his itching hand comes past,

   And their labour is all undone.

But some there be who war
With all this sinful host,
And fasten their gaze on the beautiful star
That shines on the distant coast.

And, nerving their souls for the strife,
Ever onward in silence bear,
Till they reach the home of eternal life
That looms from the land so fair.

There all is glory and love,
Beauty and brightness and mirth,
And a gorgeous canopy hangs above
This more than earthly earth.

There is no sun in the sky,
Nor sky such as we behold,
But a deathless lustre burns on high
Like the lustre of burnish'd gold.

And often upon the sea,

    When the storm bays deep and strong,

Is mixed with the tempest's maddening glee

    The sweetness of heavenly song.

For in those halls of light,

    With a wondrous witching sound,

Beautiful beings, all robed in white,

    Diffuse soft music round.

And these are they whom faith

    Hath saved from a world of woes,

And wafted over the waves of death

    To a blissful calm repose.

And happy for ever and ever

    Is he who gains that shore,

For safe by the side of the Great Lifegiver

    He rests for evermore.

RETROSPECT.

It's oh for a cot
     By the western main,
And a lowly lot
     To be mine again:
To feel as I felt
     When a dreaming boy,
And my fancy dwelt
     In the realms of joy.
When I knew no care,
     And I fear'd no foe,
Nor had thought to spare
     On a coming woe.
But morning and night
     Fresh pleasure would bring

And my face was bright
　　As a gladsome thing:
And a gladsome thing
　　Of a truth was I
In that far-off spring
　　That will never die!

I think of it now
　　With an eye tear-wet,
The passionless brow
　　And its crown of jet.
I think of it now
　　With my locks grown white,
With a furrow'd brow
　　And an eye's dim light.
I think of the change,
　　So thorough and bold;
Of the wider range
　　In the thoughts I hold:

Of a life more known
   To my fellow-men
Than it could have grown
   In the narrow glen:
And well do I ween
   That the powers I hold
Would never have been
   In the life of old.

But balance the wealth
   Of a merchant proud
With the rosy health
   Of a boy snow-browed,
And up from the scales
   Is the red dust toss'd,
And its magic pales
   By the glory lost:
And fain would I give
   All my manhood's gains

For the spells that live

   In the bounding veins,

To revel once more

   In a region fair,

With power to explore,

   And spirit to share,

In signs that are rife

   In the earth and sea,

The mystery life

   Of the things that be.

What gladness it gave,

   In the rosy morn,

Afar on the wave

   To be lightly borne !

Blown out from the land

   On the sweet spring wind,

And leaving the grand

   Old mountains behind :

Away and away,

    Right out from the coast,

Till the hills grew grey

    And the glens were lost;

Till the full white sail

    Dropt empty and free

In the lessening gale

    Of the central sea:

And the trim wee bark,

    To the eagle's view,

Was the only mark

    In the world of blue.

Sweet, too, the day long,

    My shallop to oar,

And listen the song

    Breathed round by the shore,

Where the long blue tide

    Rolls in from the sea

With its voice of pride
   And immensity:
Dim-telling of things
   In the far-off climes,
In music that rings
   Like a poet's rhymes.
And I listen'd, thrilled
   As the music grew,
Till my heart was filled
   With melody too;
And that of the sea
   Seem'd kin to my own,
And stirr'd me with glee
   As I wander'd on—

Away 'mong the rocks,
   Where the eagle broods,
And the raven croaks
   To the summer floods:

Where the downy nest
　　Of the eider-duck
Hangs high on the crest
　　Of the sea-swept rock;
And gulls on the beach
　　Have their lowly home,
Scarce over the reach
　　Of the climbing foam.
Where never was heard
　　Since the world began,
A grovelling word
　　From the lips of man;
For the wondrous gleam
　　That hallows the whole
Steals in like a dream
　　On the tranquil soul.

But more than the bliss
　　Of the morn or day

Was the stolen kiss
   When the skies were grey;
And the thrill—felt yet—
   By the waterfall,
Where the two hearts met
   That were all in all.
Come back to my heart
   O days that are gone !
And bring me a part
   Of the joy then known:
Come back, O ye days
   Of gladness and mirth !
And light with your rays
   My desolate hearth !
I'd barter a year
   Of my after-gain
To breathe in the dear
   Old boyhood again !

' THE POET AND HIS THEME.

Forever o'er the sea of song
   The poet's fairy shallop glides;
In mirth and music borne along,
   It lightly breasts the bounding tides.

From morn till night awake, asleep,
   He threads the bay, or skirts the shore;
The rolling numbers of the deep
   Are in his heart for evermore.

No stormy gust invades the calm
   That broods between his sea and sky;
But silent, low, and rich with balm
   The slumbrous zephyr wanders by.

He lives in love with all around;
  He changes as the seasons fill;
His heart—a lyre of sweetest sound—
  Is strung and swept by Nature still.

The memories of the olden time
  Are wafted to him down the wind;
He knows the songs of every clime,
  And sets them to each mood of mind.

And when the night is near at hand
  He cons them over one by one;
And far across the listening land
  The magic of his lay is blown.

He sings of life, and love, and death,
  Of all things bright and fair to see;
And in the pauses of his breath
  The waves complete the melody.

But, most of all, he loves the theme
   Of years to come when sin is dead;
Then rolls his music in a stream
   Impassioned, chaining heart and head.

For, more than all things great or dear
   The ages leave us as they roll,
This longing for the golden year
   Is centred in the poet's soul.

Oh, gentle bard, that longs to greet
   The day when all hearts throb like thine!
How many weary years must fleet
   Across the land in storm and shine?

How many loves that now are bright
   Will darken into worse than scorn
Before we burst this dismal night
   That drags us from the golden morn?

So deep the shade on hut and hall,

   So seldom glints the fitful gleam,

Alas ! I fear that, after all,

   It lives but in the poet's dream !

THORNS.

I.

The glory of sunrise
　　Fades away;
Heat mocks our weary eyes
　　All the day;
We lose the temper'd boon
　　Of the night.
For the coy, capricious moon
　　Hides her light.
Spring leaves the mountains fair,
　　But the snow
Mars their beauty everywhere
　　We may go;
If pleasure sends our bark
　　O'er the sea,

Then tempests gather dark
    On our lee.
Our souls enjoy the sweets
    Friendship knows,
But soon in vain deceits
    Friendship goes.
Do we love a maiden fair
    As the skies?
Ah, fools! we lose our care
    For she dies.
Thus morning, noon, and night,
    Land and sea,
Friendship and love unite,
    Grieving me;
The close of all my mirth
    Sounds forlorn,
And every rose on earth
    Has its thorn.

II.

The dawn is but the birth,
    Not the life;
The day should see us forth
    Fit for strife;
The birds at drowsy eve
    Seek their nest,
And mortals then should leave
    All, and rest.
If snow but failed to fall,
    Then the frost
Would blight the seed, and all
    Would be lost:
Did not the tempest's wand
    Stir the sea,
We would not know how grand
    She can be.
When earthly friendship dies,
    We should mind

That he who rules the skies
    Still is kind;
And if this death we wail
    Were not given,
Would the parted spirit hail
    Us in heaven?
Thus morning, noon, and night,
    Land and sea,
Friendship and love unite,
    Training me:
Mirth has thrill'd, ere its close
    Sounds forlorn,
And I'm grateful for the rose,—
    And the thorn.

A PLAN.

Up on the cliffs, when the morning breaks,
And the hills are bathed in a glistening dew—
When the eagle sits on the rock, and shakes
His plumes for a swim in the silent blue—
'Tis there the fresh, keen, youthful soul
With an eagle's glances hails the sun,
And the free-born heart brooks no control
When it dreams of deeds to be dared and done.

Far in the town, when the sun rides high,
And the wind blows in on the ways of men—
Where the eager crowds go jostling by,
Some seeking pleasure, some finding pain—

There does the strong heart face the stream,

    And the steadfast will work out the way,

Till the rifts and dangerous passes seem

    By the wand of a wizard enchanted away.

Down by the beach, when the daylight fades,

    And the stars shine out on the listless tide—

When the voice of the ocean alone invades

    The solitude settling far and wide—

The one true heart that has waited long

    With fond eyes piercing the dusk of the years,

Is clasped to a breast that knows no wrong,

    Though dinted with trouble and worn with

        tears.

This is the life I have planned and drawn.

    Is it well to wish it? I scarcely know.

Were it not better smooth as the lawn—

    Sweet as the scent of the rose? Ah, no.

Fain would I have Mirth alone for my mate,

But I fear that its kibes are trod by Care;

We scent the queen rose in her garden of state,

And know, although hid, that the thorn is there.

AT THE GARDEN GATE.

The moon, like a shepherdess, climbs the steeps
   Where her silent flocks of stars are straying,
And lightly down through the dark blue deeps
   Her cloudy robes on the breeze are playing:
The spell of the night is on mountain and main,
   Woodlands and waters are swathed in sleep;
And fitful and faint on the night wind's wings
Is wafted the dirge that the streamlet sings,
   As it glides through the glen to its grave in the deep.

Alone by the garden gate as I stand,
   I think of a night, just such another,
When I waited here to touch the hand
   Dear to me yet above all other:

Just so—did the moonlight tip the trees;

   Just so—the night wind rose and fell;—

Ah me ! how long should I linger now,

With the night-wind stealing across my brow,

   Ere the touch of that hand would break the spell ?

A GLIMPSE OF THE MOON.

'Tis the high noon of night, when stars should be
    bright,
  And the pale moon silent and low;
But the clouds gather black round the orb's dim
    track,
  And their shadows lie dark below:
The rain falls cold over forest and wold,
  And the brook brawls down to the sea;
There is no motion of beast or of bird,
Not the faintest chirp of a songster heard;
No light nor life on the dreary plain,—
Only the ceaseless plash of the rain
  As it rustles down through the darkened tree.

'Tis the high noon of life, when joys should be
    rife,
  And the red blood fiery and proud;
But a cloud-like pain covers feeling and brain,
  And my heart in its shade is bowed:
Care's touch strikes sharp on my soul for a harp,
  And the sound that it yields is woe;
There is no whisper of hope to cheer,
Not the faintest glimmer of respite near,
All lights of love from my ken have flown,—
Only the ceaseless rain comes down
  From the ruthless sky on the waste below.

But lo! as I speak, from the mountain peak
  A gentle gust of wind comes on,
And soft and low does it breathe and blow,
  And already the rain is gone;
The clouds fall back from the pale moon's track,
  And yonder in light she goes:

And I know that a slumbering pulse did start,

And the clouds were blown from my waiting heart,

For already the calm and the blessed light

Come down on my soul in the tranquil night,

    And spread as far as the soft wind blows.

WALLACE.

On the page of Scottish story,
  Red with valour though it be,
Who can lay such claim to glory
  As the knight of Elderslie ?
Wallace, first of all the warriors
  Ever belted blade on thigh,
May the heart that slights thy greatness
  Droop in dungeon dark and die !

Bruce was wise, and Douglas daring;
  Randolph's heart was stout and bold
Stern Kirkpatrick's sword unsparing;
  Fraser loved by young and old :

But in thee alone, proud Wallace,
  Burn'd the quenchless patriot flame:
All the rest had stooped to England,
  Borne awhile a traitor's shame.

Well their after-deeds absolved them
    From the stain that dimm'd their
      shield,
And when England's king resolved him
  They should die or meanly yield,
O how leapt each manly bosom,
  Thrill'd by Bruce's gathering cry,
And beneath his glorious banner,
  Took the field to do or die.

But in thee no stain existed,
  Oath of thine no king could claim;
Evermore thy sword resisted
  All that spoke in Edward's name.

K

How could then the doom of traitor
  Be assigned with truth to thee,
When thy soul disdained to own him
  For a king—in chains or free?

But the fools who deem'd thee traitor
  Knew not then as we know now,
That thy death has made thee greater,
  Wreath'd fresh laurels round thy
    brow:
For although to live a patriot
  Tries the strength of heart and will,
He who dies a patriot-martyr
  Proves devotion deeper still.

Spotless as the vault of heaven
  Was thy soul's untainted glow;
And to such alone is given
  Power to check the tyrant foe:

Down through all the after ages

   Beams that radiance full and clear, —

Who shall say it doth not reach us,

   Seated in our freedom here?

LITTLE THINGS.

Long have I revelled in the book of nature,
    Those wondrous pages that were penned of old,—
And sought to fathom in each varying feature
    The mystic lore its hieroglyphics hold:
And more convinced am I the more I ponder,
    That lessons meant for us are seldom found,
While we sit trancéd in a grateful wonder
    To see the everlasting wheel go round.
Though not with soul quite dead to all the glory
    That breathes around us in the open day,
'Tis but the main points of the sounding story
    We catch, blown down upon our dusty way.
The grand old hills that rear their crests to heaven,
    The stately streams that ever seek the sea,

The deep ravines with echoing thunder riven,

   The golden glory of the harvest lea,—

These all men know: but few without emotion,

   Alone within the mellow eventide,

Could pace the limit of the sounding ocean,

   Or rest upon the silent mountain side.

But though we note the lesson thrust before us

   In the long biding awe such presence brings,

We mostly fail to catch the joyous chorus

   Rung ever in our ear by lesser things.

The little flower that blooms beside the highway,

   The little brook that wimples through the glen,

The little bird that sings in every bye-way,—

   All have their little tale for heedful men.

They are the gentlest outcomings, the feelings

   With which great Nature's heart doth overflow;

They touch our sense with plaintive fond appealings

   At every corner, as we come and go.

They are the antidotes to all our fretting
 And paltry little cares of every day,
And in the heart, past chance of all forgetting,
 Memory should treasure every word they say.

LIKE THE RIVER.

O the glad voice of the river
  Flings its music round and round,
And the glen is filled for ever
  With the waters' pleasant sound;
But by neither wood nor meadow
  Will the rolling river bide—-
Never rest in shine or shadow
  Till it reach the ocean wide.

And not surer does the fountain
  Send its waters to the sea,
From beyond the distant mountain,
  Than my heart its thoughts to thee.

Other eyes may catch unwitting
　　Fitful glimpses here and there,
But to thine alone, love-litten,
　　Is my inmost bosom bare.

Far among the upland hollows,
　　When the gladsome stream was
　　　　young,
Brighter flowers adorned the valleys,
　　Louder mirth around it rung.
But through all their pride the river
　　Lightly wandered fancy free,
Till it found its home for ever
　　In the bosom of the sea.

So, in youth, I made each pleasure
　　For a while my guiding star;
Sought it as they seek for treasure
　　Late and early, near and far;

Till the silver starlets perished

On the pallid marge of day,

And the hopes so fondly cherished,

Like the stars had passed away.

Then I came, as comes the river,

Leaving all the past behind;

All the toil and the endeavour

Of the restless youthful mind.

And with calmer voice and feeling,

Here beside the peaceful sea,

To thy tender heart appealing,

Left my happiness with thee.

THE TWO GATES.

Between the present and the time to come,
  Not to be scattered till the day of doom,
Hangs, like a formless vapour, dense and dumb,
    The mystery of the tomb.

And through this mystery no eye can reach;
  But if it did, the anxious gaze would see
Two entrance gates, fast locked, to one of which
    Each man doth hold a key.

And, knowing well that two such gates are there,
  And knowing, even with our bounded sight,
Whither they tend, should it not be our care
    To form this key aright?

Alas ! how many do we see that dance
   Among the calms of life in listless sloth
Who mould it anyhow, and trust to chance
     That it may open both?

Vain chance ! one door the key so formed may ope,
   For, often used, its bars glide swift and free;
But loud it clangs behind and ends the hope
     That he might turn and flee.

But he who thinks to pass the narrow way
   Must mould his key with diligence and care,
Keep the clear metal spotless in the clay,
     And temper all with prayer.

Even to this end this earth of ours is given,
   For in the flesh we do but form the key
That opes the entrance gates of hell or heaven,
     According as may be.

A meagre faith it is of theirs who hold
    The all of man is ended when he dies;
Death's wing is but the car on which is rolled
    His soul beyond the skies.

And here, day after day, with thoughts and deeds
    He strikes the tenor of his future state,
And from the cradle sows the various seeds
    Whose ripening shows his fate.

This world is but the seed-time of his year;
    He scatters carelessly this side the grave,
But on the other, where the fruits appear,
    He gathers as he gave.

LOOKING BACK.

Is it well that the past should die?
   Should we shut out evermore
The mirth and the moan that the breeze blows by,
   From the cliffs on yonder shore?

Our bark is abroad on the wave,
   And its goal out further still;
The winds and the waters around it rave,
   And the light craft needs our skill:

Yet we pause with averted eye,
   And a boding sense of pain,
For a long, long look at the mountains high
   We never will tread again.

Ah me ! but the land was fair,
  With its pleasant woods and streams;
And memory lovingly lingers there,
  To bask in the golden beams.

For there was a light on the land
  That never shines on the sea,
Though I catch the glimpse of a snowy hand
  Still waved from the shore to me.

Even now, with mine on the oar,
  And my head half turned away,
I can see that face on the fading shore
  That flits not night or day.

And I feel as I could turn
  And bend to its spell again,
But a voice thrills through me in words that burn,
  Blown in from the misty main.

" Out on the waves is to live,
　　In the past ye only dream;
　Let it die and be lost! ye should not give
　　One glance to its witching gleam.

" If the love ye own be true,
　　Its term will outlive the grave,
　And the cherished form will meet with you
　　On the verge of the outmost wave.

" Then bend to the oar amain,
　　Till the foam breaks o'er the prow;
　Forget for a while that love lies slain—
　　It cannot be quickened now.

" But over the mist that's cast
　　Abroad on the forward main,
　There is a brighter land than the past,
　　Where love will awake again."

ONLY A DREAM.

I dreamt that the veil was drawn
  That screens the coming days,
And all the future folded there,
In the book of mystery laid bare,
  Before my wilder'd gaze.

And methought I seized the book,
  And read it page by page,
And I saw that life for me was still
A weary climb on a pathless hill,
  From youth till doting age.

There was no poet's wreath
  To ring my throbbing brow,

No sacred calm when the din was by,

Nor light to hallow the even' sky—

   All dreary then as now.

And I thought if this be truth,

   And the end is as I see,

'Tis surely a wilful waste of time

Striving to reach that radiant clime,

   Whose sweets are not for me.

Then I woke—and lo ! the dream

   Fell from me as the snow

Falls from the branch in the early morn,

When the first keen glance of the sun has

      worn

   Its hold, and it slips below.

And as the branch breaks out

   And buds in the open day,

A nobler thought possessed my soul,

When the searching light of the sun did roll

My snow-like dream away.
.

For I knew that the thing I saw

Was born of the restless brain,

And not God-sent to bear me back,

With a sense of the many gifts I lack,

Ere I a goal might gain.

So I work with earnest will,

And a heart that still hopes on;

And if no crowning wreath appears

At least I know in the rolling years

Some faithful work is done.

AUTUMN.

Lo ! the languid summer lies
 Down upon her couch of pain,
And the look that's in her eyes
 Says she will not rouse again :
Tend her well, sweet love, for you
Will mourn her all the winter through.

Was not this a wondrous web,
 Woof'd with happiness she wove,
Ere her power had reach'd the ebb,
 And her arm with winter strove ?
But she claims the gift she gave
To fold around her in the grave.

We must yield, alas! ye know,
　Ere the fields have lost their green,
I must with the summer go
　Where the wave will roll between;
But, when birds again do sing,
I will come and crown the spring.

SUMMER AND LOVE.

Was it a glimpse of the poet's doctrine
  Flushing the random thoughts that run
In the brain of the youth, that made me fancy
    Summer and Love were one?

I who had knelt at the shrine of Nature,
  Wooing her far in the lonely wild,
Till her face grew sweet as that of a mother
    Looking on me, her child.

I cannot tell how the thought did waken,
  I scarce dare hint at whence it came,
But I know that the chains they cast around me
    Fettered my soul the same.

And as I walked by the stream or mountain,
  Glimpses of her that swayed my mind
Rose up, till I saw her face in the flower,
    Heard her voice in the wind.

And then I thought, so long as the summer
  Has buds to open or gales to sigh,
I shall be rich in the lore of the lover;
    For mine will never die.

And so till the chilling breath of the Autumn
  Scattered the leaves at the root of the tree
I loitered, lost to a thought of sorrow
    Blest as few mortals be.

But now when the drear cold wind of the Winter
  Covers the earth with its shroud of snow,
I see how false is the fond resemblance
    I drew so long ago;

For the earth but rests till the Spring returning

    Shall quicken her heart to burst its chain;

But, alas! what spring will unfold the petals

    Of my dead love again?

KEEPING TRYST.

A DREAM.

O, heavens, I had a fearful dream!
　My very heart is chilled;
While sights and sounds of horror dire
　My brain with fire have filled.

I must abroad and bathe my brow
　In the cool fresh breath of morn;
For much I fear this midnight spell
　Hath left me wan and worn.

Methought that I did go to keep
　A tryst beside the sea,
In that cool grot where oft before
　My love hath met with me,

When mellow twilights wove their charm
   In melting heart and eye,
And love forgot that aught like care
   Had life beneath the sky.

But, lo ! the night I chose was not
   A night to dream of love :
Red lightnings flashed on sea and shore,
   Hurled headlong from above.

Long forky tongues shot seething by,
   And vanished through the gloom,
And thunder rumbled, peal on peal,
   In awful sounds of doom;

The mighty ocean rocked and tost,
   And tumbled in his sleep;
And many a tortured moan bespoke
   The nightmare of the deep.

Anon, like some huge monster caged,
    With far-resounding roar,
He shook his shaggy sides to foam,
    And rushed along the shore.

The lowering clouds above his head
    From east to west were driven,
Like drifting remnants of a fleet,
    Wrecked on the sea of heaven:

Till, scattering far the restless mass,
    The fearful gale that blew
Showed where the speechless moon did stand
    And whiten at the view.

And well she might, for when her light
    Did glance along the tide,
I saw a bark far out at sea,
    Her white sail bellied wide,

And bearing down with lightning speed
   Upon the sounding shore;
While high above the ocean's moan,
   And through the tempest's roar,

Oh God! I heard the voice of all
   The world most dear to me,
And loud it call'd, " I come, I come,
   To keep my tryst with thee."

Horror! I saw her near the rocks,
   The breakers foam and surge,
And forward! forward was the path
   The tempest fiends did urge.

Low down within the ocean trough
   One moment she might lie,
The next she swept like thistledown
   Far up the billowy sky.

And on before her cruel foe,
    Like a slave beneath the lash,
She spun with desperate energy
    For one tremendous dash—

For, lifted high above the foam,
    She crash'd upon the rock,
And her oak timbers shiver'd
    With the madness of the shock.

And as I fell soul-struck to earth,
    And grovell'd there and wept,
I heard the wailing voice again,
    " I come, my tryst is kept."

UNFULFILLED RENOWN.

The history of our island rings
    With praises of its great of old,
And slumbering loyalty upsprings
    Where'er their valiant deeds are told;
With swelling heart and sparkling eye
We mouth the names that cannot die.

Their fight is fought, their victory won,
    Their meed is at the hands of fame;
They win the wreath by what is done,
    And wear it, and no man can blame;
Nor do we grudge the grateful praise
That wafts their name to later days.

But who shall say that on the roll
   Oblivion hides there was not one
As mighty?—nay, a mightier soul,
   Than these dame Fortune smiled upon?
A man whose single sword and shield
Had turned the chances of a field.

Who knew the weight and worth of will,
   And prized it as all leaders do;
Nor lacked the aids of strength and skill
   To place him 'mong the favour'd few;
But whose young fame and budding wreath
Were blasted in the frost of death.

While yet the horn was at the lip
   To sound his name through all the
     land,
One fatal moment wrought a slip,
   The horn fell from the faltering hand,

And the proud prelude's opening tone
Failed in a instant and was gone.

And in the flight of such a soul
   Our loss is greater than we know,
For victory's tide unchecked may roll,
   And mighty hearts still guide its flow;
And so we hail their power with pride,
Unconscious that a greater died.

The bud that's nipt beneath the gale
   Might shape to show the fairer flower;
But whoe'er thinks of buds that fail,
   When seated in the summer bower,
Where those that braved the tempest stand,
And hallow all the fragrant land?

So with the past; great men enthrall
   The wondering gaze of after-time:

But seldom are the tears that fall
   For those who perished ere the prime.
We own their meed might not be less,
Yet yield a greater to success.

But in the world beyond the grave,
   Their guerdon will be rightly given;
The unfought combats of the brave
   Shall work their recompense in heaven;
And the nipt bud at last disclose
The beauties of the perfect rose.

TIRED.

Come to me, Sleep—for I am faint and worn;
  All night my brain hath divèd deep
For pearls of fancy to adorn
These waifs of song; until at morn,
Of all its eager impulse shorn,
  How willingly it comes to steep
  Its languor in the balm of sleep.

Come to me, Sleep—behold I cast away
  At last the book whose witching lore
Hath kept thee from thy rightful sway,
And made the night as rough as day
With toil; but thought no more will stay,

M

Its wing that late could proudly soar,

Droops, jaded with the strain it bore.

Come to me, Sleep—I have a traitor been,

But now repentant crave thy kiss;

As lover woos who once has seen

His mistress wrongly slighted, lean

I now upon thy love serene,

That sees through negligence like this,

And yields at last its balmy bliss.

Come to me, Sleep—I yield thee up my

soul,

Do with it as thou wilt; it seems

There are no arms like thine; O fold

Them softly round my frame, and hold

My head upon thy bosom old;

For happiness my spirit deems

Nowhere but in thy world of dreams.

O! gentle Sleep, I feel thy kindly glow.

   I feel thy balmy presence near;

Already faint the noises grow

That sound so fitfully below,

One after one the last lights go,

   And I who neither see nor hear

   Have comfort in another sphere.

SONGS.

BACCHANALIAN SONG FOR THE
NEW YEAR.

Fill the cup and let it circle
    Freely round the festive board;
Night without may storm and darkle,
    Here her madness is ignored:
For with wine that beads before us
    What for raving night care we?
Let us raise the sounding chorus,
    And be wilder yet than she.

Do not nights like this one strengthen
    Hearts that long in tears have lain,
And with links of brightness lengthen
    Memory's reach of rusty chain?

Life would ne'er be crown'd with
   pleasure
If we let such moments go,
When there's that in every measure
   Floats us from the reefs of woe.

Wine was made to charm our sadness,
   Nights like this to own its sway;
Surely 'twould be worse than madness
   All its sweets to cast away:
Let it flow as free as ocean!
   And while hand is joined in hand,
We will empty with emotion
   All our cups at love's command.

Pledge we first the souls departed
   In the year that now is fled;
Who so base or canker-hearted
   Would not bumper to the dead?

Those we loved—may heaven bless
    them!
    They are free from every woe;
For the rest—we can but wish them
    Firmer friendships where they go.

Pledge we now the living present
    With its mingled shine and shade;
May these hours we find so pleasant
    Graff'd in memory, never fade;
Pass the glass, and let it smother
    Petty spleen in royal glee;
Come, get up, and all together
    Drain it out with three times three!

Last, with neither roar of pleasure
    Nor in boding silence dumb,
We will fill the brimming measure
    To the year that is to come;

Ah, my friends ! there is no knowing

What this future may contain,

But behold, the goblet's flowing— '

Let us drain it out like men.

LAYING BY A LITTLE FOR A RAINY DAY.

Hey, bonnie lads, that are lippen-fou o' siller,
    Ye that trow the lift o' life has ne'er a clud for
      you;
But live sae pack wi' Fortune ye're as guid as bairns
      till her,
    And hing upon the dimples o' her mou'.
Haud a wee, my lads, or sairly she'll beguile ye,
    Dinna think a' the year can be as blythe as May;
But while it's in your pow'r ne'er let your pleasures
      wile ye
    Frae layin' by a little for a rainy day.

The wild hill bee that ye meet amang the heather,
    Though he sings awa' the simmer in its balmy bell,

Has wit eneugh to guess there's an end to bonnie
    weather,
  And pangs his winter stores in mony a cell.
Then when the snaw comes, and bitter winds are
    roarin',
  Little will it fash him suld the drift smoor the brae,
Among his gowden kaims like a king he'll be snorin'—
  His honey has been hoordit for a rainy day.

Far be't frae me e'er to stint the young o' pleasure,
    Aneath its cheery sunshine they are baith gude and
      fair;
But just a kennin' less in the reamin' daily measure,
    Wad mak but little differ here or there;
And gey puir comfort it gies to man or woman
    To ken they've wastit chances they ne'er again can
      hae,
To see the simmer's pride fa', and dreary winter comin',
    And ken they've naething hoordit for a rainy day.

JEAN: A LYRIC.

Few are the flowers on Wanlock braes,
   And wondrous tiny those that be,
For nights of storm and sunless days
   Keep down their growth on moor and lea;
But though the hills be stern and bare,
   And flowers are few and far between,
One peerless blossom still is there,
   Rose of the wilds—its name is Jean.

Nursed in this lonely glen, my heart
   Has borne like it few things of joy,
But chiefly lived its life apart
   From love of man and maiden coy

But though its golden dreams are rare,
  And in their glow few shapes are seen,
One face forever lingers there—
  One queenly form—its name is Jean.

And Wanlock braes, despite this dearth
  Of leaf and petal, scent and show,
Are dear above all braes on earth
  Where buds of beauty thickly blow;
Nor does my heart in wailings loud
  Mourn o'er a happier might-have-been,
But dwells apart, content and proud;
  Would'st know the charm?—its name is Jean.

ATWEEN AND MENNOCK-HASS.

Atween and Mennock-hass
   There is a cosy biel',
Whaur a bonnie lad and lass
   Micht haud a tryst fu' weel;
And gin ye like, May Moril,
   As sune's the gloamin' fa's,
Ye're free tae share my plaidie there
   Frae every blast that blaws.

The muirlan' may be bare,
   And snell the norlan' breeze—
Little shelter rises there
   Save what yon craigie gies;

But in my heart, May Moril,
   There is a blythesome glow,
And tae't sae fain I'll fauld your
    ain,
   That cauld ye'll never trow.

We'll hear the lintie sing
   His sang o' love and pride,
Blabbin', silly, thochtless thing,
   O' joys he canna hide.
But sweeter far, May Moril,
   And tae nae ear but thine,
I'll whisper lown, hoo ye hae stown,
   The heart that ance was mine.

I canna brag o' gear,
   Tae cleed and keep ye fine;
Rough and raploch mountain cheer
   Maun please gin ye'll be mine.

But pree and pruve, May Moril,
   And think or ye decide;
There's few sae fiel as them that biel'
   Ayont a shepherd's side.

IN LOVE.

I think of thee, when morn bestows
Her kiss upon the waking rose;
When song-birds carol, clear and loud,
High up beside the sunny cloud:
And sure those sights and sounds so rare,
The very freshness in the air,
Give new delight and joy to me,
Born of the touch they take from thee.

I live for thee, when man with man
Is working out the fated plan;
When fears and hopes, and woes and joys
Distract the sense with jarring noise;

And in the melee, ringed with foes,

More fiercely fall my eager blows,

Because that in the end I see

Their weight will hew my way to thee.

I dream of thee—when night hath hung

Her chain upon the gladsome tongue

That cheer'd us in the rosy dawn,

When light was clear on lake and lawn:

And though the dreams that come be sweet

As ever fell at mortal's feet,

I fling them from me, glad and free,

And wake again to life and thee.

HALF-PAST TEN.

Half-past ten on a mirksome nicht!
 Ochone! but the time hings drearily, drearily;
The lift is ableeze wi' the fireflaucht's licht,
 And the hoolet is skirling eerily:
I carena tae dauner by glen or brae,
 I canna look brisk or think cheerily,
For the laddie that lo'es me is far, far away,
 And oh! but my life wags wearily.

Half-past ten last spring was a year,
 And Robin was ever and aye beside o' me;
I tentit nae sorrow when he was here,
 And dule, care, and girnin' seemt fleyd o' me:

But noo I'm alane the lang winter e'en,

    When ilk lass meets her jo sae cheerily;

And the saut tear comes rowin' adoon frae my een,

    For oh! but my life wags wearily.

Half-past ten's wearin' on tae twal,

    And winter'll bluister awa' intae May again;

And Robin'll come wi' the lamb tae the faul'

    And comfort my heart wi' his stay again:

But noo I am feckless the lee lang day,

    I canna look brisk or think cheerily,

For the laddie that lo'es me is far, far away,

    And oh! but my life wags wearily.

THE DAYS OF OLD.

In the brave days of old, ere the falchion formed the
plough,
When courage steeled his sinew 'neath the banner
and the brand;
When the haughty crest of chivalry was free to every
brow,
And prowess was the test in every land:
O! then the heart was chainless as the wind,—
The mighty soul of freedom scorned to pawn its
pride for gold;
And manliness and glory were the mottoes of the
mind,
In the brave days of old.

In that grand reign of right, never coward kept a
crown,

Nor cunning conquered valour with the supple guile
of brain;

For the iron heel of honour held the wily serpent
down,

And majesty was master in the main:

Then love and truth were foremost in the fight,—

The smile of blushing beauty was the guerdon of the
bold;

And the victor's brow was laurell'd in his king and
country's sight,

In the brave days of old.

But that bright sun hath set, and the night that gathers
round

Is alive with all iniquities that batten in the gloom;

And vainly does the poet seek to sanctify the ground

With flowers that are but scattered o'er his tomb.

We hear no more the stirring trump and drum
  That cheer'd the eager warrior when the strife around
    him roll'd:
And the sweetest sounds that greet us are the memories
    that come
  From the brave days of old.

O! would that we might wake, as from a hateful dream,
  To wed the noble purpose that our ancestors have
    shown;
Our barks are ever drifting down upon a golden
    stream,—
  Wealth is the only standard that we own;
For it we pledge the dearest hopes of life,—
  Brain and sinew, nay, the future of the soul is often
    sold:
And we seek it as the warrior sought his glory in the
    strife
  In the brave days of old.

I PU'D A ROSE.

I pu'd a rose in Mennock wuds
   No lang sin', on my road gaun hame,
A mossy sprig wi' twa bit buds,
   Ye'd barely think deserved the name;
But graff'd acqueesh a sproutin' tree,
   And eithly tentit e'en and morn,
As bonny a blossom opened ee
   As ever busk't the laden thorn.

I woo'd a lass on Wanlock braes,
   A winsome birkie, bauld and slee;
Whase life gaed by like summer days,
   Wi' lauch as licht and heart as free:

But sune the lowe that winna hide

    Gart Tibby's een grow wondrous fain,

And syne I saw wi' joyfu' pride

    Her heart was graft'd acqueesh my ain.

AT THE TRYST.

The dew is hanging heavy on the rose,
  The wind is stealing softly through the tree,
And every gentle breath that comes and goes
  Stirs the daisy's dimpled bosom dreamilie:
At the stile where we so oft with joy have met,
  To-night we meet to kiss a long farewell,
And often will the eye of love be wet
  With the memory of this parting in the dell.

In yon elm the crooning cushat cheers her young,
  Deeper through the wood the throstle calls,
And my heart, in tune with Nature's happy tongue,
  Could answer with its eager throbs and falls;

But, ah! the light is fading off the stream

    That slips its weary waters o'er the lawn,

And my soul must cower closely round its dream

    In the night that comes, and hunger for the dawn.

A little while, and we were all so glad,

    And now—the very thought o't dims my eye—

A little while, and we will both be sad,

    Oh! were not love so hopeful I might die.

But though we part at present, we'll forget

    In the years that come with gladness, this farewell,

And we'll laugh and chase the merry moments yet

    By the stile that sees us parting in the dell.

GIN YE LO'E ME.

Gin ye lo'e me, lassie, meet me
    Up the Wanlock glen at e'en,
Where the wimplin burnie wanders
    Through amang the knowes sae green;
Where the bonny bloomin' heather
    Sweetly scents the muirlan' air;
I will tell ye o' a secret,
    Lassie, gin ye meet me there.

Ill wad set sae saft a story
    Tae be tauld in open day,
Wi' your thrawart minny glowrin'
    Owre ilk dawtie word I say;

But when e'enin' cranreuch airts her
　　Tae her couthie ingle-en',
Meet me, and I'll tell ye something
　　Some fowk wad be fain tae ken.

In the gloamin' glen the mavis
　　Tells his mate how leal he loes;
A' forenicht the hills o' Wanlock
　　Hear how blithe the linty woos;
Ilka bird then nestles closely
　　Tae some ither heart as kin',
But I'll never pree their gladness
　　Till ye come and comfort mine.

THE LAST TOAST.

One more cup ere we rise from the board
    Where we sit in the daylight so dim,
Let the last ruddy drops of the vintage be poured,
    And bumper each bowl to the brim!
We drank to our Queen and our Fatherland too,
    While corks lay undrawn on our shelves;
But this is the last, and give each one his due,
    Let the last toast be this—to " Ourselves."

    Then, here's the last toast of the night,
        For we've drained every flask on the shelves,
    Get up, then, and drink it with meaning and
           might,
    And let the toast be—to " Ourselves.

England's Queen—we are proud, are we not,
  Of the deeds that ennoble this name?
And we pray that the dastardly coward be shot
  That ever speaks light of her fame.
But Queens, at the best, are but seen from afar—
  Little more of this earth than the elves;
Their glory comes to us like light from a star;
  But we—we are facts to Ourselves.
      Then, here's the last, &c.

Scotland's hills of the heather and thyme
  Are dear to the hearts of the true,
And fondly we yearn in a far away clime
  To bring the wild peaks to our view;
But chiefly they're dear from the worth of their sons—
  From the prince to the peasant that delves,
And how do we know but this quality runs
  In a trifling degree in—Ourselves?
      Then, here's the last, &c.

PAIRING-TIME.

I heard the muirhens in the dawin',

   And siccan a rippet they raised!

Sae crousely the muircocks were crawin',

   I glowert as the birds had been crazed;

For I thocht that the hamely employment

   O' biggin' a nest had been quiet;

But gin it can yield sic enjoyment,

   What say ye, young lassie, to try't?

The muircock is blithe wi' his dearie,

   A' nicht in the howe o' the hill;

But lang were the gloamin' and eerie,

   If spent on the muir by himsel':

And what is a man withoot woman,

    But a muircock that hasna a hen?

Sae bide wi' me noo in the gloamin',

    And shorten my nicht in the glen.

A cozy wee cot and a cannie,

    Is ready whenever ye will,

Weel plenished wi' plenishin' bonnie,

    And wantin' for nocht but yoursel':

Then come in the gloamin', my treasure!

    For troth I am weary tae ken,

Gin pairin'-time brings the birds pleasure,

    What wonderfu' joys it gies men.

THE DEATH-SONG OF TIME.

In the empty years that loom upon the world
   Ere the mountains shall be levell'd with the sea,
Or the blackening bolt of thunder shall be hurled
   From the caverns of the life that is to be,
Mute and haggard on the margin of his power,
    'Mong the nations that are crumbling in his
      shade,
Robed in all the passing splendour of the hour,
   Time is leaning like a warrior on his blade;
And he feels the sickly flaring of the sun,
   Hears the slogan of the breeze that rushes past,
And marks the ebbing ages as they run
   Among his fingers, wearing quickly to the last;

Then, rising to the fulness of his form,

    He passionately clamours to the throng,

And louder than the roarings of the storm

    Comes the music of the mighty wizard's song:—

" Get ye hence and be forgotten! Who are ye

    Clinging wonder-stricken round the skirts of Time?

Have ye left your homes in idleness to see

    The shadow that will blast ye in your prime?

Do ye think the lion leaves his cave to die,

    That the meaner beasts may triumph in his

        pain?

Though the light be fading surely from mine eye,

    It will burn till yours can never glint again!

" Mine arm hath been against ye all my days,

    I have conquer'd, and will conquer to the end;

There is no mortal force that ye can raise

    But the iron guard of Time will turn and bend.

Ye are not what ye were no more than I,

    I have worn away your nerve and sapp'd your

        will;

It is not long to linger—surely I

    That have borne so long can bear a little still.

" O the tooth of dull decay hath toucht the hills,

    And soon their flaunted pride will be no more,

" And wearily the wrinkled ocean spills

    The weepings of his dotage on the shore;

All things which were of old are waxing grey,

    And if such things as these can cease to be,

What hope have ye, the insects of a day,

    To wrestle through this weary war with me?

" It is not many days that I must wait

    Till the fulness of your time be come and gone,

I will leave ye, drawn together, to your fate,

    And the spell will settle o'er ye one by one.

Man and matron, prince and peasant, young and

old,

The coward's dust shall mingle with the brave;

Many flocks are penn'd together in a fold

When the world is not a dwelling but a grave.

" And when ye walk no more upon the earth,

And your feet have left no traces where they trod,

When the stately halls that echoed with your mirth

Are not left to tell the future your abode;

When the very name of man has been forgot,

And all the fierce emotions of his prime,

The longings and the labours of his lot

Are like mists upon the memory of Time;

" When the mountain and the meadow shall be one,

And the glamour of the glen hath ceas'd to be;

When the mystery of the midnight and the moon

Cannot rouse the slumbering madness of the sea;

When the sun that shines so feebly shines no more,

 And the primal darkness settles o'er the deep,

I will push my silent shallop from the shore,

 Glide away into Eternity—and sleep!

I WOO'D MY LOVE.

I woo'd my love in the merry spring time,

 And O! sae cheery sang the laverock frae the sky;

Wi' the world fair before me and my spirit in its prime,

 Never laverock held a heicher head than I.

I won my love in the lang simmer day,

 And O! sae sweetly sang the lintie on the lea,

An' my heart—as blithe's the lintie's—had but little

   thocht o' wae—

 Heaven seemed tae ope its gowden gates to me.

I lost my love in the dowie back-en',

 And O! sae sadly sang the mavis on the hill:

Hoo I warslet through the autumn by mysel' I hardly
    ken,
    Never herriet mavis dreept sae lane and chill.

I mourn my love a' the hale winter through,
    And O! sae lanely sings the snawbird in the snaw;
But the bird will whistle bonnie when the simmer sky
        is blue,
    And my weary heart maun break, or hear it a'!

EL DORADO.

Where is the land of the sunlight and shadow,
　Rivers of silver and mountains of gold;
The beautiful province yclept El Dorado,
　Imaged erewhile by the dreamers of old?
Seek it no more where the sounding Atlantic
　Murmurs its mystical tales in your ear;
Come, I will show you the region romantic!
　Listen, the true El Dorado is here.
　　A silent wind from a far blue sky,
　　　A bark on the lake in the clear moonshine,
　　The first look of love in a merry blue eye,
　　　And a dear little hand in mine.

Say not 'tis false that the country we live in,

    Old mother England, the free, may contain

The peace and the plenty for which ye have striven,

    Deeming them far in the orient main;

Back from the lands of the sun to our valleys!

    This is the haven to which ye should steer;

The light and the gloom of the magical palace—

    Treasures uncounted and countless are here:—

        A silent wind from a far blue sky,

          A bark on the lake in the clear moonshine,

        The first look of love in a merry blue eye,

          And a dear little hand in mine.

Love is the "sesame" that opens our nature,

    Gifting our vision with power to behold

The fair face of earth, with a smile on each feature,

    Making it truly a region of gold.

Come, then, ye hearts that with longing are weary,

    Think not the world is faded and sere,

Much that we know may be gloomy and dreary,

But surely the true El Dorado is here: —

A silent wind from a far blue sky,

A bark on the lake in the clear moonshine,

The first look of love in a merry blue eye,

And a dear little hand in mine.

THE BURN'S ANSWER.

Bonnie burn, that rins
   Tae the roarin' sea,
Hae ye no a word ava
   Frae the hills tae me?

Ye row'd by a shiel,
   In a far-aff glen,
Whaur a bonnie lassie bides
   That we baith suld ken.

For aft hae we roved
   By your bosky braes;
Ye tentit a' oor love dream,
   Its joys and its waes.

That gowd glint o' heaven
Ye never wad forget.
O, tell me, bonnie burnie,
Is her heart mine yet?

The bonnie burn grat.
"O, bairn! I wad fain,
Bring the news that ye spier for,
To cheer ye again:

"That shiel in the glen
Still stan's by my side,
And the lang and bosky howms
In their simmer pride;

"But the lass—wae's me!—
She's a wife lang syne,
And the gowd dream has faded
In your heart and mine;

" There's nocht yonder noo

    Brings gladness tae me,

And I'm fain tae hurry by

    Tae the roarin' sea."

SCOTLAND'S CHARMS.

O lightly laughs the sailor lad
   That knows my pride and me,
And straight he speaks of wondrous lands
   Beyond the sounding sea;
But never a tale I've heard him tell
   Could force my heart to own,
There ever were hills like Scotland's hills,
   Where Freedom has fixed her throne.
      Then here's to the hills of Scotland,
        Where the heather is waving free,
      There are no hills like Scotland's hills,
        Nor any so dear to me!

O proudly boasts the soldier bold,

    Who shows a victor's scars,

That none can match the dauntless foes

    He faced in foreign wars;

But something more than a soldier's boast

    Should force my heart to yield,

There ever were men like Scotland's men

    Drawn up on a tented field.

        Then here's to the men of Scotland,

            Wheresoever their footsteps stray,

        There are no men like Scotland's men,

            No nation so bold as they!

O softly sighs the gallant gay,

    For some dark beauty's smile,

Whose charms still keep his fancy fixed

    On her lone flowery isle;

But say, shall an idle gallant's flame

    Have power to make us know

There ever were maids like Scotland's maids,

As far as the winds can blow?

Then here's to the maids of Scotland,

With their eyes of the heaven's own blue,

There are no maids like Scotland's maids,

No hearts that are half so true!

A SONG OF PAIN.

Turn me aboot wi' my face to the wa',
　　O mither, till I dee!
I canna look intae your een ava
　　That wont to be dear tae me:
I want to be dune wi' the licht o' day
　　And the weariesome fauchts o' life,
For little o' pleasure or promise hae they
　　To the mither that ne'er was a wife.

Gie me a kiss or a heartenin' word,
　　O mither, or I gang!
Ye mind hoo ye ca't me your winsome bird
　　Lang syne when I kent nae wrang:

And never had I sic need o' your love
  In the far away time as noo:
I hae nane but yoursel' and the God above,
  Whase mercy I'm fley'd tae sue.

Comfort the bairn I'm leavin' ahin',
        O mither, when I'm gane!
The puir thing 'ill thole for his mither's sin
  As bitterly as his ain;
And dinna be hard wi' his faither, min',
  Suld he come when I am awa',
But think on the joyfu' days lang syne,
  When he liket me best o' a'!

REAR OUR FLAG ON HIGH!

Rear our flag on high!
　That gift which Freedom gave,
'Twill stream above our victory,
　Or shroud us in the grave.
There's pride of heart and strength of arm
　Rank'd at the guns below,
And he that weens to work it harm
　Must be a dauntless foe.

Rear our flag on high!
　And when it flies unfurl'd,
Mark how it stands against the sky,
　And seems to dare the world!

The light winds proudly lift its folds
     And toss them far and free,
And forth the good ship fares, and holds
     Old England on her lee.

Pour your choicest wine,
     And pledge the vessel round,
And pray that she may plough the
     brine
For years with timbers sound:
In peace or war, in shine or storm,
     Unconquered as of yore,
With England's banner standing firm
     Through all the tempest's roar.

Then, should Heav'n decree
     This flag of ours must fall,
In terror men may look to see
     The dismal end of all;

And even in that hour 'twill seem,
    When sinks the vessel low,
To flutter on the 'whelming stream
    In triumph to the foe!

SERENADE.

When the moon is bright in heaven,
 And her spell is o'er the sea,
One little hour might sure be given,
 Dear love, to me!

In the blaze of wealth and splendour
 It is thine to pass the noon,
Where gallants crave in accents tender
 Thy meanest boon.

But though day doth keep us parted,
 When the light hath left the lea
Night joins again the faithful-hearted;
 Come then to me!

Well I know how true and fondly
    That young heart of thine doth beat,
And in the glittering crowd thinks only
    When we may meet.

Meet me now: I do not ask thee
    Favours in the gaudy day;
I know 'tis right thou then shouldst bask thee
    In pleasure's ray!

Still among the fair be fairest,
    I am proud to see thee shine;
But hold the hour I reckon dearest
    Apart, as mine!

Evening's quiet hour that finds thee
    Stript of regal robes and glee,—
For thy soft, gentle look then binds me
    Closer to thee.

Life hath much of pain and sadness

In its depths for those that live;

But mine are swallowed in the gladness

Such moments give.

SONNETS.

POESIE.

Whence comes the charm that broods along thy shore,
    O sunny land of song?   What potent thrall,
    Reckless of ocean's rise, or flow, or fall,
Holds us about thy marge for evermore?
Here, where the long wave breaks in measured time,
    And fills our being with its rhythmic moan,
    From far inland the glories of thy zone
Burst on our view, and beckon us to climb.
Shades of the mighty dead! whose snowy towers
    Stud the deep gorges and the wooded braes,
Is there no nook for cots so small as ours?
    No tree whereof we yet might gather bays?
But to be with thee, and to hear the wave
Roll music round the land, is all we crave.

GLOAMING.

The hinmaist whaup has quat his eerie skirl,
   The flichtering gorcock tae his cover flown;
   Din dwines athort the muir; the win' sae lown
Can scrimply gar the stey peat-reek play swirl
Abune the herd's auld bield, or halflins droon
   The laich seep-sabbin' o' the burn doon by,
That deaves the corrie wi' its wilyart croon.
   I wadna niffer sic a glisk—not I—
Here, wi' my fit on ane o' Scotland's hills,
   Heather attour, and the mirk lift owre a',
   For foreign ferly or for unco sicht
E'er bragg'd in sang; mair couthie joy distills
   Frae this than glow'rin' on the tropic daw',
     Or bleezin' splendours o' the norlan' nicht.

LOVE.

Where is the height at which the poet's soul
   Will cease to soar? beneath the boundless sky,
   By sea or shore peaks do not point so high
But it may scale; or by the frigid roll
Of Greenland's waters, or the desert lone
   Of utmost Ind; in calm, or cloud, or storm,
   Earth opens to its "sesame" kind and warm
The hidden beauties of its every zone,
Then with a limitless survey like this
   Tell me, my heart! what magic doth thee thrall
   That thou canst find a comfort more than all
Earth's wonders yield in one slight maiden's kiss?
O reckless heart! dost think thou findest there
The charm that keepeth these forever fair?

FAME.

In the cool watches of the silent night
  My soul was wafted to the land of dreams
And moved in ecstacy of calm delight
  Along the margin of its silver streams.
With raptured eye it saw the bright array
  Of goodly gifts for mortals held in store,
  And, faint with passion, hunger'd more and more
To win some token of its favoured stay.
" Choose what thou wilt," a passing voice did call;
  At once my spirit made a snatch at Fame,
But with the bauble in its grasp did fall,
  Nor ever after could its ground reclaim.
Alas! that wish of mine should yearn to clasp
A gawd that brings such troubles to the grasp.

GLENCRIEVE.

Is this Glencrieve?—I deem'd the spot more fair
　　When here we lingered many years ago,
　　My love and I, and watched the ruddy glow
Of sunset deaden on the moorland bare.
Perchance some path my erring foot hath ta'en
　　That led astray, and I have missed Glencrieve,
　　Then will I back, for I am loth to leave
These hills till memory be stirred again.
Yet stay! this is the glen—yon glint so bright
　　Smites the long upland and its summit hoar
　　　Just as it smote them then; but I, alone,
Here, in the shadowed gorge, have lost the light
　　Of eyes whose lustre robed the scene of yore
　　　In a dim loveliness for ever flown.

APRIL.

There's not a month in all the rolling year
   So true to life as April; sun and shower
   Change rule so quickly that the trembling flower
Begins to smile before it sheds the tear.
In me as well some darker hours of fear
   Mix with the lightsome joy that fills the day,
But less and less these cloudy thoughts appear,
   Sweet winds of hope do waft them all away;
Already in my soul the breath that brings
   The bud and blossom has been gently blown;
   And at its touch awaken'd thought has grown
Beyond the limit of these sluggish springs:
So blow, sweet wind! and clear the sky above
And all my soul will blossom o'er with love.

BANISHED.

As some lone dweller in a distant land
   Chooseth to linger by the restless sea,
   And counts the leagues of shifting waves that be
Between him and his home, while fancy's wand
Brings for one moment to his gloating view
   The happy times that he can know no more,
Then blinds him, weeping—till each scene he knew
   Fades on his eye along the dismal shore,—
So I, forever banished from thy presence, feel
   A momentary gladness in the thought
   That eyes so bright as thine at one time brought
Heaven down to me, and glow'd to list my weal.
Alas ! for broader than the exile's sea
'S the gulf now stretched between those eyes and me.

HEROISM.

Not only in the time and garb of war
   The hero breathes; not only now and then
   We catch bright glimpses of this man of men,
The labour of whose hands is nois'd afar;
But even now, in these degenerate days,
   As noble hearts do beat as those that bore
   The invader backward in the days of yore,
And earn'd the guerdon of a deathless praise.
Wherever human hearts do war with wrong,
   Or maiden virtue shuns the fowler's guile,
Where honest hands to humble toil belong,
   Or wealth assists the trodden poor to smile—
There throbs a soul which wins the highest claim
To ring—remembered—in the song of Fame!

DISCONTENT.

There's not a bliss in all the joys we clip
    Can match the charm of those in whose rich glow
    We clothe the future—joys we never know,
Yet long so much to finger that we slip
Substantial pleasures lying round our feet,
    For these same glimpses, beckoning far away,
Which, when we chase, as speedily retreat:
    No charm we hold can bid their brightness stay.
We reach the spot where all was deemed so fair,
    From yon far mountain where we made our moan,
    But ah! the gleam that lit the land is gone,
And the lone moorland stretches waste and bare;
    While onward still, amid the gathering gloom,
    Flits the weird glow that wiles us to the tomb!

BLUEBELLS.

We note the standard of a nation's mind
   In England's queenly rose; it breathes of power
   And beauty, pride, and all the generous dower
Of lavish nature, and is meet to bind
Among the tresses on a regal brow.
   Strange, then, that roses only bloom for me
   As fairest flowers; they move me as the free
And kindling glance of beauty moves me now,
Wedded to her I love, no more; but thou,
   Bluebell! scarce seen beside the rose, thou hast
An influence other than the short-lived glow
   Of pencill'd petals, for the slumbering past
Wakes at thy smile, and makes me inly pine
For bonnie Scotland's hills—thy home and mine.

SINGING.

To-day I heard a singer in the crowd
   Discourse sweet melody, and could not choose
   But stand and listen; for that she did use
The gift she bore by Nature's hand endowed
So sweetly, and her notes both low and loud
   Thrill'd with such passion that I could not pass,
But paused, half conscious that my heart avowed
   A sudden yearning for the comely lass:
And in that thrill of sympathy I knew
   That here was one whose maiden soul was flung
   In all its richness thro' the lay she sung,
And here, if still on earth, one heart was true;
And mine had been apart from such so long
It bless'd the wanderer for her welcome song!

ROMANCE.

O that some touch of elfin power might glance
    Along the strings of this my lowly lyre!
    That more than mortal ardour might inspire
This song of mine to thee, far-famed Romance!
Lone land, upon whose tracts no sun doth beam
    That heats our nether globe, though faint and far
    The mellowed lustre of one drowsy star
Yet haunts thy limit with its hallowing gleam—
(The star of song).   Against thy faery shore
    Its rays are rolled, as the long tide is rolled
Against the unconscious beach for evermore;
    While we—rapt watchers—through the gloom behold
Thy wondrous heights, and long therein to soar,
    And scatter broadcast all the gems they hold.

REALITY.

Star-struck, and throbbing with such thoughts as these
 I turned me towards the town; for all night long
 With poet frenzy I had timed my song
To the deep swinging of the listless seas.
And O, my God! what creatures found I there
 To listen lore like this; in vice grown bold
 And misery mad, their haggard features told
Their higher need. My dream dissolved in air,
And in its stead this thought engrossed my mind—
 That if the poet's mission be to bring
Earth nearer Heaven, a way more sure and kind
 Than prating starry nonsense is to fling
One ray of light upon the wretched, blind,
 Seared souls that thread the dark streets grovelling.

R

LOVE-WEARY.

What shall I do (love being dead) to bring
    Back to my heart the rapture and the joy,
    The glorious fancies of the dreaming boy
That made my early life eternal spring?
Red lips, soft eyes, the spell of woven arms—
    All these have failed, embraces are grown cold,
    Eyes thrill me not as they were wont of old,
Nor at the red lips touch my bosom warms.
I am love-weary; come, O radiant Spring,
    And in the lonely places wake delight,
For I at large would fain be wandering
    With thy glad presence evermore in sight;
Thence might I turn upon the world to prove
Thy touch doth make a substitute for love.

SPRING.

Who has not felt thy witching presence, Spring?
    Upon the mountain top and in the glen
    Thy rapid coming is foretold to men
In diverse ways: the wandering breezes fling
Gladness around us in our outs and ins:
    Aloft, the opening sky is deeply blue,
    And the bright orb of morning glistening through
Smiles on the fearless songster that begins
To hail thy reign: the earth, no longer coy,
    Arrays herself as might a beauteous bride,
While smiles and songs of mirth reveal the joy
    And fulness of her wondrous mother-pride.
O happy man unto whose heart these bring
The dewy freshness of thy spirit, Spring!

GIFTS.

If I unto my kindred dust should go,
　　With but one gift of fortune, and that gift
　　Of my own choosing, do ye think I'd lift
A longing eye on wealth, or worldly show,
Or beauty, or the higher meeds of fame?
　　No! one by one I'd set these gifts aside
　　As scarce worth having, and with poet-pride
I'd wreathe this chaplet round my deathless name:
One little song—one little rapturous lay,
　　Simple, perhaps, and sad, but true to all
The best in Nature, of which men would say,
　　" Here truly is a charm whose linkèd thrall
We may not break—it breathes the heart's pure play,
　　And till this ends it cannot pass away."

PLEDGED.

Friends, I have sworn a vow.   The terrible bond
   That Jephtha, flush'd with vict'ry, register'd
   Was not one whit more certain to be heard
And sealed in heaven, than this one now beyond
My revocation; and although to his,
   In point of magnitude or pain to keep,
   Mine be as streamlet to the boundless deep,
Yet, calmly pondered, it amounts to this—
That in the judgment of Almighty God
   And interest of my particular soul,
   This bond requires fulfilment just as whole
And faithful as that found: therefore beware
   Lest ye should swerve me from the narrow road,
And mar a heavenly covenant unaware.

HOGG.

Lift up thy radiant welcome, Scotland! here
  In lowly garb one of thy truest sons
  Is bent before thee; love of country runs
Not stronger in the peasant or the peer
Than in the heart of him thy laggard pride
  Is slow to own.   And if true love like his,
  And the rich welling of such music is
Lost on thy parent ear—what cave will hide
The unnoticed strains my feebler spirit sings
  For love of thee?   Insulted Coila yearns
To see him seated on the throne that springs
  At the high footstool of his master, Burns;
Then grant the boon, and let affection see
Thy ploughman and thy shepherd knee by knee!

NATURE.

The sweetest intercourse of kindred souls
    Is not all sweet: harsh words will intervene
    To mar their joy, as o'er the blue serene
Italian heaven a black cloud often rolls,
Flinging long glooms on earth; so all that springs
    'Tween man and man at best is incomplete;—
    Bitters flow close upon his choicest sweet,
And love, like riches, is not void of wings.
But with the constancy that doth belong
    To every motion of the moon-drawn sea
    My heart is led in willing thrall of thee—
Spirit of Nature, whose sole voice is song!
In whose pure love nor hitch nor flaw doth bide,
But rolls for ever an unbroken tide.

L'ENVOI.

Dear Jack, the posie is made up I pull'd—
    The wild hill blossoms wrought in wilder rhyme;
    Is there aught in it has the scent of thyme
And freshness of the moors? or has my spirit, school'd
In deadening cities, lost the power to throw
    Their natural charms around the scenes we love?
Mayhap it has; yet would I have thee know,
    Nature was still my theme; the gentle dove
Mourns not her absent mate with moan more sad
    Than I, pent in the smoke these cheery days
    At losing her; and O if any lays
Of mine do breathe her music, I am glad!
And in contentment leave them at thy feet,
Knowing thy heart will own that music sweet.

www.ingramcontent.com/pod-product-compliance
Lightning Source LLC
Chambersburg PA
CBHW030640030726
47497CB00006B/1873